BITTER CREEK RANCH

Now owners of the Bitter Creek Ranch in Wyoming, Butch Cassidy and The Sundance Kid have swapped robbing banks and trains for a more relaxed pace of life. Or so they think . . . For when sisters Rosa and Louisa Jordan come to the ranch, trouble quickly follows in the form of their stepbrother Abe Gannon. The violent outlaw is tired of living in the shadow of Butch and Sundance, and wants to teach them a lesson . . .

Books by Saran Essex
in the Linford Western Library:

TRAIL TO VENGEANCE

SARAN ESSEX

BITTER CREEK RANCH

Complete and Unabridged

LINFORD
Leicester

First published in Great Britain in 2015 by
Robert Hale Limited
London

First Linford Edition
published 2017
by arrangement with
Robert Hale
an imprint of
The Crowood Press
Wiltshire

*A catalogue record for this book is available
from the British Library.*

ISBN 978–1–4448–3309–6

Published by
F. A. Thorpe (Publishing)
Anstey, Leicestershire

Set by Words & Graphics Ltd.
Anstey, Leicestershire
Printed and bound in Great Britain by
T. J. International Ltd., Padstow, Cornwall

This book is printed on acid-free paper

For Colin, the two dads,
the two mums,
Dino and Tex,
and Bruno and Bob

1

Bitter Creek Ranch, Wyoming was situated a few miles north of the middle fork of the Powder River, and in the Big Horn mountain country in a remote, secluded area surrounded by diverse scenery.

The land around the ranch was interspersed by flat, open ranges, rolling hills, cool streams, and treacherous, winding canyons.

It was roughly twenty miles to the east from the red, sandstone wall shielding the outlaw hideout of Hole-in-the-Wall.

The nearest towns were Buffalo, about two days' ride to the north, and Casper, which was about three days' ride to the south.

Approximately halfway between the ranch and the town of Casper was a general store and blacksmith shop, the properties of brothers, Jasper and Jesse Sheldon.

The owners of Bitter Creek Ranch were the outlaws, Butch Cassidy and The Sundance Kid.

The ranch had been left to them by a friend, Nathan Casey, who had passed away.

Butch and Sundance raised cattle and horses on the ranch. Some of the horses they sold to the outlaws at Hole-in the-Wall, and some to other ranchers in the area. The cattle they bred were a hardy, Hereford breed imported originally from England and much sought after by other ranchers. Butch and The Kid mostly sold the cattle to the other neighbouring ranchers. The cattle they did not sell were driven to Cheyenne and then taken by train to the stock markets to be sold. The outlaws hired drovers for this task. They had four resident ranch-hands to help them on the ranch, and an old out-law friend named Hank Westwood who helped them out with the other jobs, such as cooking, cleaning and washing. They would hire other ranch-hands to help them out when they needed it.

They also acted as unofficial guards for the outlaw hideout of Hole-in-the-Wall; they kept a discreet lookout whenever it was possible to do so for any suspicious-looking strangers or lawmen who might try to enter the hideout, and in return the outlaws did not try to steal any of their cattle or horses.

Lawmen had tried a few times to enter Hole-in-the-Wall, but they had always been beaten back by the outlaws, and had not tried for over a year to infiltrate it.

Butch Cassidy had at one time been an outlaw leader of a gang at Hole-in-the-Wall. He had organized the successful robbing of banks and trains and was known as a smart thinker.

For the last twelve months, though, Butch and The Sundance Kid had spent all of their time, energy and effort on looking after their ranch. They were experts, with cattle, guns and horses.

Before his death, Nathan Casey had fenced in the boundaries of his ranch land.

He had not used barbed wire for the fencing, but timber.

Riding along slowly, and checking the timber fencing around one of the huge enclosures where the cattle were grazing was Harry Longbaugh, alias the tough and fast-shooting gunman, The Sundance Kid.

Riding alongside of him was a pretty young female. Aged about seventeen, she had a slender figure, and long, thick and glossy dark auburn hair. She wore a light green shirt and a long brown riding skirt with a wide belt. Her name was Rosa Jordan, and she lived with her sister, Louisa, and her stepbrother, Abe Gannon at the outlaw hideout of Hole-in-the-Wall.

Abe Gannon was the leader of a very violent outlaw gang, and he was angrily against both of his stepsisters spending so much time on the ranch of Butch and Sundance. One of his reasons was that he thought of the girls as his children to do with what he liked. He treated them like servants. He would even hit them at times. Another reason was that

4

he despised and resented Butch and Sundance.

When Butch and Sundance had been residents of Hole-in-the-Wall, they had been very protective of Rosa and Louisa, and very helpful to them whenever they could be, and ever since they had left the hideout to take up ranching, their friendship had been deeply missed by the two girls, which is why Rosa and Louisa spent so much time with them on the ranch.

On finding a break in the fence, Sundance dismounted to fix it. The break was near to a fence post and a sharp, jagged piece of the fence rail was sticking out.

Rosa remained seated on her horse facing him and watching him. It was obvious from the way that she looked at him that she liked him a lot, but The Kid had failed to notice her feelings.

The Sundance Kid was six feet tall and aged in his late twenties. He wore a wide-brimmed Stetson, black shirt and black pants, and a black bandanna around his neck. He had sandy-coloured hair which flopped down over his forehead. His eyes were a steel-like grey-blue colour, and were for most of the time devoid of any expression. He had a tanned complexion and attractive facial features which most people usually failed to notice because he did not smile too often. A thick sandy moustache adorned his upper lip, and the lower half of his face was frequently covered in unshaven stubble. His body was long and lean, but well-muscled.

Sundance had a well-deserved reputation as being very fast and skilful with a gun. He loved difficult and dangerous challenges, and he was a hard man to beat in any kind of fight. He had faced the toughest and fastest of men and had always won. Sundance never liked to lose at anything. He had been born in the East, and had run away from home at a very young age to seek adventure. He had travelled West and had been looking after himself ever since.

With a hammer and nails, Sundance began to mend the break in the fence.

The cattle in the enclosed pasture

carried on munching the grass. They were branded with the letters BC followed by a slash mark. It was the brand of the Bitter Creek Ranch.

While hammering in the nails, The Kid suddenly became alert as he heard the thundering sound of horses' hoofs getting ever nearer. He also heard Rosa utter a startled cry.

Sundance left the hammer and nails on the ground and straightened up. He saw Abe Gannon and two members of his gang from Hole-in-Wall riding towards them.

The three men reined in just a short distance from where Rosa still sat on her horse facing The Kid, and from where Sundance stood near the fence.

Abe Gannon was a mean-looking, heavy-set man. He had thick black hair and a beard. He gave the outward appearance of being very formidable.

Rosa's face paled slightly at the sight of her stepbrother, but she had a lot of spirit in her and she tried not to show her growing fear.

Ignoring Sundance, Gannon stared fiercely at Rosa, and snarled out, 'You shouldn't be here, girl, your place is with me!'

Fighting back her fear, and looking defiantly at him, Rosa said, 'You don't own me. I can be where I like!'

'You'll ride back with me now!' Gannon cried out, and he urged his horse up closer to her.

His nearness alarmed Rosa, and she tried to pull her horse further away from him, and in doing so she kneed her horse forward, and closer towards Sundance.

Gannon's two gang members, tall and lanky Walt Austin, and burly Jimmy Kenner, slowly moved their horses into positions to one side of Gannon, and facing Sundance. Their hands were hovering near their gun holsters as though warning Sundance not to interfere.

Abe Gannon turned his fierce glance to Sundance. 'Is Louisa here too?' he barked out.

'She might be,' The Kid answered coolly in his usual quiet, but very strong, expressive tone.

Louisa was, in fact, back at the ranch house with his partner, Butch, but Sundance did not say so.

Gannon glared angrily at The Kid; he knew that Sundance was a dangerous man to cross, and that he could only be pushed so far. There was a very vicious streak in The Sundance Kid.

At Hole-in-the-Wall, Butch and Sundance had very often shown their dislike at the way that Abe and his gang had treated Rosa and Louisa. They had even come to blows on several occasions, and Butch and Sundance had not been the ones to back down.

With all this in his mind, and with his hatred of The Kid in his eyes, Gannon snapped furiously at Sundance, 'You shouldn't be encouraging them here!'

Sundance did not answer him straight away. Gannon did not frighten him, and neither did his two gang members. The Kid had a completely fearless nature, it was one of the few things that he had in common with Butch.

When he did answer Gannon, Sundance spoke quietly and with a dangerous undertone in his voice. 'Don't you try telling me what I should or shouldn't be doing, Abe,' he said. 'You should know better than that.'

Sundance felt sure in his mind that he could handle the developing dangerous situation. He was sure that he could handle any situation. He had total belief in himself and in his abilities. Nothing daunted The Sundance Kid.

Walt Austin and Jimmy Kenner, who were watching him with their hands hovering near their guns did not worry him at all; he knew that he could draw his gun and kill all three men before they could move if he wanted to.

'You surely can't want a gunfight,' Gannon grinned with malice at him, 'not so close to your cattle.'

He was hinting at spooking the beasts and causing a stampede.

Sundance gave no reply, he was a man of few words, and he just stared impassively at Gannon.

The cattle that Gannon was referring to had been trained as best as was possible by Butch and Sundance to get used to most noises, including the sound of gunfire. The two former and skilled rustlers had patiently and gradually familiarized the beasts with as many loud noises as they could.

'And,' Gannon went on, he was still giving his malicious grin, 'if you want to take me on in some other way,' he looked at his two men, 'well, there are three of us, and you know us, Kid, you know how tough we three are.'

Sundance smiled with amusement. 'Do I?' he asked. 'I don't recall any of you ever coming out on top in any of our past fights at Hole-in-the-Wall.'

The eyes of Walt Austin and Jimmy Kenner suddenly seemed to glow with anger.

Gannon's face turned red, and he spat out, 'Well, then you had your partner to help you, didn't you?'

Sundance kept his amused smile and said, 'It was still three against two, or were

11

there more of you?'

There were five usual members of Gannon's gang, and all of them had been involved at some time in minor brawls with Butch and Sundance.

Austin and Kenner were seething with anger at The Kid's words and amusement, and were eager to draw their guns and open fire on him.

Gannon turned to look at his two men, and he saw the eagerness in their eyes, but he shook his head at them. He wanted to think over his options. He was fully aware that there were three of them, and between them they should be able to deal with one man and a girl, but he knew that even an army would have trouble dealing with someone as deadly and as tough as The Sundance Kid.

Gannon, though, felt averse to the idea of just riding away and letting Sundance think that he had won, so he decided to take some course of action. He was close enough to Rosa to reach out and grab hold of her horse's reins, and that was what he did. He started to pull on them.

Rosa was alarmed at Gannon's action and tried to pull the reins free of his grasp. She pulled with such force that the beast became fearful. It whinnied shrilly and reared up on its hind legs. Rosa struggled to control the animal, but before she could get the horse under control and its forelegs back on the ground, it struck out forcefully with its front legs and kicked Sundance in the chest, and sent him crashing backwards through the fence rail. The back of The Kid's head luckily missed colliding with the fence post by inches but he gashed the left side of his forehead on the sharp, jagged piece of wood that he had been attempting to mend as he fell though the fence rail. Blood gushed out of the wound.

Sundance lay sprawled out on the ground, but he was still conscious.

Rosa instantly pulled out a gun that she had hidden down her wide belt, and fired off a shot in panic.

She was not used to handling a gun, and her shot went wide, blazing across the pasture, and narrowly missing one of the cattle that was grazing there.

The cattle began to mill about nervously, making low growling sounds.

Rosa's shot had disturbed them.

Austin and Kenner jerked their guns out from their holsters and aimed them at The Kid, but before they could open fire, Sundance beat them to it.

The Kid's forehead was cut and bleeding, and he was still on the ground, but he had pulled himself up into a sitting position, and in one rapid movement, too fast for the eye to follow, he had drawn his Colt, aimed upwards, and fired two shots at Austin and Kenner.

Both men emitted cries of pain and dropped their guns. They clutched at their bullet-graze injuries and cursed. Walt Austin was injured in the forearm, and Jimmy Kenner in the wrist. Both wounds were only superficial and bleeding slightly.

The milling of the cattle grew stronger, and their growling sounds grew louder.

Cursing savagely, Abe Gannon pulled

out his gun.

Sundance was on the alert and ready to shoot again, but he did not have to.

There was the sound of fast galloping, and two male riders appeared on the scene from the direction of the ranch house which was just over two miles away.

In a whirling cloud of dust, the two riders pulled their horses to a stop close to Gannon and his men.

They both held guns in their hands, and one of the men called out threateningly to Gannon, 'Try to fire that gun, Abe, and you're dead!'

Gannon had his finger on the trigger ready to fire, but he hesitated.

The rider who had called out to him was Sundance's partner, Robert Leroy Parker, alias the former outlaw leader, Butch Cassidy, and he was not bluffing. Butch was almost as fast and as accurate with a gun as The Sundance Kid.

Butch did not like violence or killing, but when it came to his partner, then it was different.

The two men had been partners for

15

just over seven years, and in spite of their many differences, the two outlaws had an unbreakable bond, and had saved each other's lives.

Their bond had been forged by circumstances rather than personal feelings. During their time as bank robbers and train robbers while residing at Hole-in-the-Wall, they had been through a lot of dangerous situations together, and had eventually gained each other's trust. They were now like kin to each other and as close as two people who shared a kindred spirit could ever hope to be. Amazingly, they would even give their lives for each other.

Abe Gannon was wise enough to realise that he had no chance against the two former residents of Hole-in-the-Wall. Sundance aimed at him from the ground. Butch was close enough to almost touch him and he still had his Colt aimed at Gannon.

The young man who had ridden up with Butch had kneed his horse over to the other side of Rosa while covering

Gannon and his two men with his gun.

'Drop the gun, Abe,' Butch ordered sharply, 'and raise your hands!'

With an angry grimace, Gannon dropped his gun, and very reluctantly raised his hands. He stared at Butch and Sundance with loathing. He had resented them for a long time. He resented their success as bank and train robbers, he resented Sundance's obvious speed with a gun and Butch's smart thinking. He also resented their fearless natures.

Butch glanced at The Kid, who still sat on the ground covering Gannon with his Colt. Blood was running steadily down the left side of his face from his gashed forehead.

'You OK, partner?' Butch asked.

'I'm fine,' Sundance answered him in a curt tone. 'You know I could have handled them.'

Butch grinned. He was used to Sundance's curt manner, and he knew without any doubt that his partner could have handled the three men, just as he knew that Sundance could handle almost any situation no matter how dangerous. Butch had been a witness to this many times during their partnership.

Butch Cassidy was five feet eleven inches tall. He was also aged in his late twenties. His body, like his partner's, was long and lean, but very wiry. He had pleasant, attractive features, and striking, kingfisher-blue eyes. His hair was light blond and wavy. He had a warm and friendly nature, and was well liked by nearly everyone who knew him. He was almost always cheerful and smiling. Total strangers were drawn to his happy, friendly personality, and to the mischievous twinkle in his compelling blue eyes.

He was dressed in a blue shirt and dark blue pants. He wore a wide-brimmed hat, and a blue bandanna around his neck.

He had been born in Circleville, Utah, the son of an English father and Scottish mother, and he was the eldest of thirteen children. He had worked on a farm near to his home until, at the age of seventeen, he had walked out on his family. He had become bored with his life and wanted some excitement and adventure.

He had also walked out on a girl named Amy Bassett. She had been the daughter of a neighbour and he had loved her since the age of seven.

At times, he was overwhelmed with feelings of guilt for leaving his large family and Amy.

'I know you could have handled them,' Butch said mildly to The Kid while flashing him a friendly smile, 'but you're hurt, and a little help is OK, isn't it?'

'I ain't hurt!' Sundance snapped. 'It's just a scratch, that's all!'

Butch sighed as he looked at his stubborn partner. The wound was clearly more than just a scratch. The blood was still running down The Kid's face. Butch knew that The Kid would much rather suffer than ever admit that he was hurt in any way.

Pride and stubbornness, Butch thought to himself were two of The Kid's worst faults.

Butch next turned his attention to the

young man who had ridden up from the ranch house with him.

That young man was Johnny Latham. He worked for Butch and Sundance on the ranch. He had previously worked for Nathan Casey.

Like Rosa, Johnny was aged about seventeen; he had blond hair and a cheeky grin. He was also the son of US Marshal Joe Latham.

Unlike the marshal, Johnny was good natured and likeable. He did not have much to do with his father.

Marshal Joe Latham was a mean, unscrupulous man, disliked and distrusted by many. He had let it be known across the country that his main mission in life was to capture Butch and Sundance.

Johnny was very attracted to Rosa, which was one of the reasons that he had urged his horse up next to Rosa's mount, and while still holding his gun on Gannon and his two men, he asked her if she was all right.

Rosa gave him a nod and a weak smile. She was more upset about

Sundance getting hurt than about anything else.

'Johnny,' Butch said to the lad, and indicating Gannon, Austin and Kenner with his gun, 'please escort these three men off our property. They can maybe have their guns back later.'

'Gladly,' Johnny smiled.

Two more ranch-hands, brothers, Tim and Tom Turner, rode up to join them, and they offered to go with Johnny to help escort the three men off the ranch.

Gannon lowered his hands and with a glare at all of them, started to ride away with his two wounded men and his escorts, calling back angrily, 'This ain't over, Butch!'

'I hope not!' Sundance yelled in answer to him. If Gannon wanted more trouble, then he would happily give it to him.

Butch felt an inner foreboding; he hated the thought of any more confrontations with Abe Gannon, but knew it was probably inevitable. He put his Colt back into his holster, and then dismounted to help his partner to his feet.

The gash on Sundance's forehead was hurting him and blood still flowed down the side of his face, and his chest ached from the horse's kick.

He still held his Colt in his right hand. The gun was impressive. It had a mother-of-pearl grip, and the initials S.K. were carved on the grip.

Still sitting astride her horse, Rosa looked anxiously at The Kid. 'I'm sorry about my horse kicking you ... ' she started to say.

Sundance looked angrily at her and said harshly, 'Don't you ever fire a gun unless you know how to use it. You damned near shot one of our herd and started a stampede!'

Rosa's face fell at his angry words, hot tears sprang to her eyes, and she wheeled her horse round and quickly rode away.

Butch had spotted her tears, and unlike Sundance, he had noticed that she had feelings for his partner. He frowned as he watched her riding away. He knew how badly Sundance's words had hurt her. He also knew that another one of

Sundance's worst faults was his quick and mean temper.

'Don't you think that was a bit harsh, partner?' Butch asked The Kid quietly.

Sundance replaced his Colt back inside his holster. 'But it was true,' he snapped, 'and I tell it like it is. If she don't like it, then tough!'

Butch knew that his partner always said what he thought, and he would not have him any other way. A one-off was how he always thought admiringly of his partner, but The Kid's directness was sometimes hurtful and inappropriate. Even Butch's feelings had been terribly hurt many times by The Kid's cold, un-thinking words.

Butch took a look at The Kid's wound; there were a few wood fragments mixed in with the blood. Butch carefully picked the fragments out and cleaned up the wound as much as he possibly could using his bandanna, he then wrapped his bandanna around The Kid's head.

Sundance winced at his touch.

Butch smiled and said, 'Just a scratch,

is it?'

Sundance grunted a reply.

Butch finished fixing the break in the fence.

The cattle had quietened down again and were happily munching the grass.

Butch grinned with satisfaction as he watched the animals. 'Hey, partner,' he remarked to The Kid, 'I guess all that time we spent in trying to get them used to gunfire paid off.'

'Yeah.' Sundance gave him a faint smile, and then, feeling proud of their achievements with the cattle and the ranch itself, they shook hands.

They mounted their horses to ride to the ranch house.

They kept their horses at a slow pace, mainly because Butch was worried about his partner's forehead wound, which Sundance kept insisting was nothing. They passed a corral which held about ten horses. They were Quarter Horses, which the outlaws bred and trained.

They trained the horses to work with cattle and to get used to having a rider on their backs.

Butch still felt upset for Rosa. He knew how much she liked The Kid, and how badly her feelings had been hurt, and he felt that his partner had been too hard on her, so he said to Sundance, 'Instead of having a go at Rosa, don't you think that you should maybe have offered to help her to learn how to use a gun properly?'

Sundance suddenly pulled his horse to a stop, and stared hard at Butch. 'I should have what?' he snapped.

Butch also brought his horse to a stop. He and Johnny had seen Rosa's attempt to shoot Gannon, and he said quietly to The Kid, 'Rosa was scared when she fired that gun. Abe scared her and she tried to defend herself as anyone would. I was thinking that maybe you could give her some lessons in how to handle a gun.'

'Why me?' Sundance demanded. 'Why not you?'

Butch smiled, he was well aware that he had to be careful in what he said next. Sundance was obviously still annoyed with Rosa, and not ready to listen to reason.

'You are the perfect person to train Rosa,' Butch said mildly as he tried to work his charm on his partner. 'Not many people can handle a gun the way that you do.'

The Kid's eyes flashed in anger. He was unimpressed by Butch's words, and said sharply, 'Flattery don't work on me, *amigo*, you should know that, and neither does your charm.'

Butch took a deep breath. When he used his charm he could usually get anyone to do anything for him, but not Sundance — his stubborn partner knew him too well.

Butch was not giving up. 'OK,' he said brightly, 'I'll put it another way, I'll tell it like it is. Gannon will most likely have another go at trying to get Rosa back, and she needs to know how to defend herself, so if you give her some training with a gun, she might hit her target next time.'

Sundance stared at him with some suspicion, wondering if Butch was up to something, and he asked again, 'Why me?'

Butch saw his wariness, and said, 'I ain't got no hidden motive in mind. I'll train her if you won't, but you were too hard on her, and I know that you won't apologize to her … ' He broke off and looked hopefully at his partner.

Still staring at Butch, Sundance read his mind and said quietly, 'So you think I should teach her how to use a gun instead.'

The partners were able to read each other's minds with a natural ease.

'Yeah,' Butch grinned.

Sundance went quiet and thought it over. The wound on his forehead was starting to throb. He did not really see why he should apologize to Rosa or teach her how to improve her shooting skills. She had almost caused a stampede and got him killed, and he was about to voice all of this to Butch, when Butch said with a weary sigh, 'She was scared, Kid, can't you understand that? And she is a friend of ours.'

Butch had read his partner's thoughts. Sundance said nothing. The throb from the wound was getting worse.

Butch noticed that his partner was in pain, and he decided to give up on his idea to help to mend Rosa's hurt feelings. He gave his horse a nudge and a gentle command, and started the animal off at a trot towards the ranch house. Sundance rode slowly after him.

The ranch house was in sight of the two outlaws when Sundance said in a very curt tone, 'She almost got me killed, you know.'

A look of concern crossed Butch's face, and he said contritely, 'Sorry, partner, forget what I said. I shouldn't have suggested it — '

'No, you shouldn't!' Sundance snapped, but then he said in a more moderate tone, 'But you're right, she is a friend of ours.' The two men always stood by their friends. 'I'll give it a try, I'll give her some training in how to use a gun, but I won't treat her with kid gloves.'

Butch grinned to himself. Rosa was a feisty one, she would not expect kid glove treatment.

They rode up to the stables to the right of the ranch house, and despite protests from The Kid, Butch helped him down from his horse. They took their horses into the stables and saw to the animals' needs. Sundance started to feel a bit light-headed and Butch took hold of his arm to support him as they walked towards the ranch house.

The ranch house itself was a strongly built two-storey timber structure with a large porch attached to the front. Yards away from the house and on each side of it were log buildings. There were barns and stables and a bunkhouse with a cook-shack attached. There was also a well for the water that they used.

To the rear of the ranch house was a range of tree-clad, low-lying hills. About half a mile to the right of the ranch house flowed the narrow and rock-strewn Bitter Creek after which the ranch was named and which they also used for water at times. The banks of the creek were lined with trees and boulders.

Butch and Sundance entered the ranch

house and Hank Westwood, their old outlaw friend, a man in his sixties who helped to cook and clean for them, boiled up some water and sat Sundance down. He removed the blood-stained bandanna that Butch had wrapped around The Kid's head and started to clean up the wound with the help of Rosa's sister, Louisa.

Hank had some medical experience. He had left the medical profession to become an outlaw. He had been a member of an outlaw gang at Hole-in-the-Wall, but not Butch's gang. The gang that Hank was involved with mainly concentrated on rustling.

Hank was small in height. He was very thin with greying hair and pale blue eyes. He had been a friend of the two outlaws when all three of them had been staying at Hole-in-the-Wall. He had left the hideout to join Butch and Sundance on their ranch.

The ranch house had two large rooms downstairs and three bedrooms upstairs. Downstairs there was a large kitchen with a cast-iron stove, and a large living room with a brick-built open fireplace. The wooden furnishings, tables, chairs and shelves were mostly handmade by the previous owner of the ranch, Nathan Casey.

Butch, who could turn his hand to anything, had made some extra cupboards for the kitchen. The floors were timber with large hand-made rugs covering them.

Hank decided that Sundance's wound needed some stitches. Butch and Louisa left Hank to it and went outside on to the porch where there was a wooden bench, rocking chairs, a sofa, and a table and chairs. They sat down on the bench. It was late afternoon and a light breeze was blowing.

Sitting so close to Butch caused Louisa's heartbeat to quicken with excitement, because just as Rosa liked The Kid, she liked Butch Cassidy, but she had an unexplainable feeling that his heart belonged to someone else.

Louisa was older than her sister, nineteen and very attractive. She had a slim figure and long, wavy, dark blond hair. She wore a blue blouse trimmed with lace, and a long black skirt. She was quieter and steadier than the spirited Rosa, but the sisters were very close.

'Rosa was here just before you rode in,' Louisa said. 'She told me about Abe grabbing her horse's reins, and her trying to shoot him. She's gone for a ride now, she wants to be alone for a while. She feels bad about Sundance getting hurt and about firing her gun and almost shooting one of the cattle.'

Butch smiled. 'Well,' he said gently, 'I don't think she should feel too bad about it. She was scared and she acted out of fear, and she's had enough punishment for it from Sundance's angry tongue.' He suddenly laughed. 'You know, getting a lashing from Sundance's angry tongue can hurt worse than a bullet wound.'

Louisa smiled, then something in Butch's mischievous blue eyes compelled her to laugh, and she wondered again, as she had done so often in the past, how two such different people as Butch and Sundance could have such a strong, unbreakable bond.

'Although,' Butch added seriously and more to himself than to Louisa, 'I'm real glad that Sundance was not hurt more badly than he was.'

Butch then turned to smile at Louisa again, causing her heartbeat to quicken more and her inner excitement to grow, and he said quietly, 'I don't think that you and Rosa should go back to Hole-in-the-Wall tonight; it'll be too dangerous for you with the mood that Abe is in. You can both stay here on the ranch until you find somewhere else.'

Louisa smiled warmly at him. 'We already owe you and Sundance so much,' she stated. 'We've caused you enough trouble … and we'll be putting you in more danger.'

'That's rubbish!' Butch scoffed. 'You and Rosa are our friends, and we always stand by our friends.'

Louisa smiled at him again, and then said sadly, 'The trouble is Abe thinks that he owns us, but we are not even related to him by blood. His mother married our father, and when they both died of typhoid, Abe took over looking after us. He took us to live at Hole-in-the-Wall with his frightening outlaw gang, and he treats us like servants. He even hits us at times.'

Butch said gravely, 'You have to get away from him, Louisa, that's the only way you'll have a chance of a decent way of life.'

2

A day later, to Rosa's surprise and secret delight, Sundance took her for a ride with him. They were a few miles away from the ranch and riding through a range of wooded hills, when he pulled his horse to a stop and told her that he was going to give her a lesson on how to use a gun.

There was a visible mark on his forehead, and the stitches which Hank had applied had not yet been removed.

He first got her used to the basics of handling a gun, and the workings of the weapon.

He then set up a target for her on a tree that was shaped similar to a cross. He hung a coat on the outstretching branches, and nailed a thick wedge of material to the wide trunk.

'OK,' he said quite abruptly to her, 'just think of this tree as a man and aim for the widest part, which is the chest.'

He pointed to the wedge of material to indicate that it was the chest part. 'And then, after you have fired at him, move out of the way fast.'

'Move out of the way?' Rosa asked.

'Yes,' Sundance emphasized, 'move and move fast. You might miss your target and he will be shooting back at you, so once you have fired your first shot just move, and with a bit of luck, that way he won't hit you.'

'Do you move out of the way?' Rosa asked out of interest.

'I don't have to,' Sundance answered without any hint of boasting in his voice. 'I don't miss my target.'

They practised for most of the morning; Sundance would not give her any time to rest. She had to keep firing at the tree until he felt satisfied with her shooting.

He was not too friendly with her, and he snapped at times, but Rosa did not mind, she was just happy to be with him.

On the ride back to the ranch, Rosa

tried to start a conversation with him, and found it hard work.

'I am grateful to you,' she began, 'for helping me to improve my shooting.'

'It wasn't my idea,' was Sundance's gruff reply, and that was the end of the conversation as far as he was concerned.

Rosa tried to start another conversation with him, and asked him if he liked ranching.

'I wouldn't be doing it if I didn't like it,' he replied curtly.

Rosa then asked him how long he thought he might stay on the ranch and run it.

The Kid did not like talking about himself or his future, and he told her to stop asking questions.

They continued the rest of the ride to the ranch in silence.

The huge red sandstone wall that guarded the entrance to the outlaw hideout of Hole-in-the-Wall, stretched over thirty miles in length, and the wall shimmered in the distance in the radiant mid-morning sunshine as Sundance rode a young Quarter Horse that he was training alongside a winding and shallow stream.

It was four days after Rosa's first shooting lesson.

Sundance dismounted to let the horse drink. The V-shaped pass in the red wall that led to the narrow canyon entrance to Hole-in-the-Wall was located about five miles to the west of him.

There was still a mark and a huge bruise to the left side of his forehead, but the stitches had now been removed.

As the horse drank from the shallow stream, The Kid became aware that two riders were thundering towards him from the direction of the pass.

They were galloping so fast that dust and gravel was flying up from their horses' hoofs.

As the riders got closer to him, Sundance realized that they were Rosa and Louisa, and he cursed softly to himself.

The girls were still staying on the ranch

with the Kid and Butch, and Sundance guessed that they had ridden to Hole-in-the-Wall to fetch some things. Butch had previously told them not to go to the hideout alone.

Rosa and Louisa had galloped almost level with The Kid when he saw that their faces were full of fear. They did not seem to realize that he was there and were about to gallop on past him when he called out to them.

On hearing his voice and suddenly recognizing him, the girls brought their horses to a stop a few feet away, but they did not appear to want to hang around too long, and were casting anxious glances back at the pass leading to Hole-in-the-Wall.

Something or someone had obviously frightened them.

The Kid walked over to them, he saw that they were panting.

'You two idiots!' he snapped. 'What the hell do you think you are doing? Butch told you not to come to Hole-in-the-Wall alone!'

'I know he did!' Rosa responded

sharply to him while trying to control her panting. She still looked very frightened, but her eyes showed a defiant glow. 'We are not idiots, we thought we'd be OK, we chose to go today because we know that it is the usual day that Abe and his gang are away in Casper!'

'Oh, really?' Sundance snapped angrily and sarcastically. 'Then what are you afraid of?'

It was Louisa who answered him in a shaky voice. 'Ginger Moran was there,' she said. 'He tried to stop us from leaving; we managed to get away from him, but he is following us.'

The Kid knew Ginger Moran. Ginger and his cousin, Rocky Moran, were members of Abe Gannon's gang. The cousins both had reputations for being fast with a gun. They were tough and violent men, and they would not hesitate to kill or beat up anyone, including young ladies like Rosa and Louisa.

Sundance turned to look back at the pass and saw another rider pounding across the rough ground towards them.

He knew that the rider was Ginger Moran.

'Ride back to the ranch,' he told the girls in an even voice.

Rosa hesitated. She felt worried about him; she knew that he intended to take on Moran.

'Now!' Sundance yelled at them.

The girls spurred their horses into a fast gallop away from him.

Drawing his Colt, Sundance aimed at Ginger Moran as the gunman pounded towards him, and then he stepped right into his path.

'Stop right there, Moran!' he yelled.

Ginger Moran, so named because of his mop of red hair, pulled his horse to a shuddering stop a short distance away from Sundance.

'Get out of the way!' he snarled. 'I want those girls, not you!'

'You have to go through me first,' The Kid told him calmly.

'You don't scare me,' Ginger snarled again.

'And you sure as hell don't scare me.'

The Kid gave a chilly grin.

'Those girls belong at Hole-in-the-Wall with Abe!'

'They are no one's property.' The Kid spoke with icy calmness. 'They belong where they want to be.'

Ginger cursed as he looked into The Kid's cold eyes and into the muzzle of his Colt. They had known each other for over four years, from both of them being members of outlaw gangs at Hole-in-the-Wall, and they had experienced a few clashes before.

'Do you expect me to back down?' Moran demanded, his face showing his fury.

The Kid gave a short, mirthless laugh. 'I expect nothing; the next move is yours.'

Ginger said furiously, 'Let me get down off my horse and then we'll settle this.'

'OK, get down.'

Sundance kept his gun on Ginger as the gunman dismounted.

Moran stood a few feet away from Sundance. He had two holsters attached to his gunbelt, one on each of his hips, and he had a gun in each holster. He kept his hands still, but close to the two guns.

Sundance calmly holstered his colt, but he kept one eye on Moran's hands as he did it.

The two men faced each other.

No emotion showed in Sundance's eyes. He had trained himself from an early age to hide any emotion that he felt. Only Butch ever knew what he was thinking or feeling.

Anger glowed vividly in Ginger's hazel eyes. He felt that The Kid and Butch had interfered too often in how Abe and his gang treated Rosa and Louisa, and he also had a deep resentment of the success of Butch's outlaw gang in their bank and train robberies and the way that they had always forced him to back down at Hole-in the-Wall.

The seconds ticked away as The Kid and Moran faced each other.

Moran's hands hovered closer to his two guns.

Sundance watched him with a

confident, half-smile, feeling certain that he could easily beat Ginger to the draw. He did not believe in losing at anything. He watched Ginger's eyes.

As Sundance watched him, Moran slowly and carefully started to move to the left; he was aware that the sun was behind him, and he wanted to position himself so that the bright sun was directly behind him and that The Kid's view of him would be blurred by the sun's brilliant glare.

The sun's intense radiance dazzled The Kid, and he had to move his head at the same moment as Ginger's hands dived for his guns.

Ginger drew, levelled, and fired his guns almost in one action.

As soon as Ginger had started to move to the left, The Kid knew what the gunman's intentions were. He knew that the sun was behind Moran, and even as Sundance moved his head and his eyes out of the sun's glare, he dived to the ground and rolled to the side, drawing his Colt at the same time.

Moran was still firing with both guns,

but his shots were rushed. His first bullets had missed their target because of The Kid's fast actions in diving to the ground and rolling out of the way.

Bullets were blazing the ground around The Kid, sending small pieces of rock flying into his face.

Sundance's gun roared only once. A bullet smashed through the skull of Ginger Moran, and he fell dead.

Sundance was training Rosa to aim for the widest part of the body, but he was sure enough of his own shooting skill to fire a bullet into a part of the body where he thought that it would do the most harm when it mattered.

Slowly, Sundance got to his feet, his face scratched and bleeding. He checked that Moran was dead, then he climbed up into the saddle of the Quarter Horse to ride back to the ranch.

The Kid was riding along a faintly defined trail with huge masses of rock and clumps of brush on either side, and he was about ten miles away from Bitter Creek Ranch when he saw another rider galloping as fast as the rough trail would allow towards him. He smiled on recognizing the outline of his partner. He guessed that Rosa and Louisa had reached the ranch, and that they had told Butch about Ginger Moran. He pulled his horse to a stop and waited for his partner to ride up to him.

On seeing The Kid, Butch's face broke into a broad, relieved smile, and he slowed his horse down and brought the animal to a stop close to The Kid.

Butch stared anxiously at The Kid's cut face, and remarked, 'I guess Ginger tried his tricks.' He had complete faith in Sundance's skill and speed with a gun, but he still worried when his partner got into a gunfight.

'He tried,' Sundance said impassively.

'Are you OK?'

'Sure,' Sundance answered abruptly. 'You worry too much — you're worse than a mother hen.'

'And Ginger Moran? Or need I ask?'

Sundance gave a faint grin. 'He won't be troubling anyone again.'

Butch said almost apologetically, 'I never expected the girls to go to Hole-in-the-Wall alone. They told me they were just going for a ride... ' He seemed to blame himself for what had happened with Moran.

'It wasn't your fault,' Sundance spoke with annoyance, 'and anyway, *amigo*, we can't expect to avoid trouble with Abe Gannon and his gang, not while we are helping Rosa and Louisa, and if one of us had gone with them to Hole-in-the-Wall, Ginger Moran would still have had to be dealt with, wouldn't he?'

'Yeah,' Butch said resignedly. He knew sadly that more trouble was to be expected. Abe Gannon would not be too pleased about what had happened to Ginger Moran, and neither would Ginger's cousin, Rocky.

The rickety open wagon with the four occupants aboard being pulled by two fine and strong-looking, black horses rumbled to a stop outside of the general store of Jasper and Jesse Sheldon on a warm and bright Wyoming morning.

A few yards up from the store and on the same side of the street was a blacksmith shop.

Jasper Sheldon was the blacksmith while his brother Jesse looked after the store. They were also in the process of opening up a saloon. The building was already erected and supplied with some spirits, whiskey and kegs of beer, but was not yet fully operational. It was located just yards past the blacksmith shop, and just beyond the not yet functioning saloon were some other buildings.

Jasper and Jesse Sheldon were gradually building up their own small town.

The terrain surrounding the general store and upcoming town was rough and varied. There were large areas of grassland, canyons and rocky hills, intermingled with creeks and streams. The Powder River flowed nearby.

The four occupants of the wagon climbed out of the vehicle.

They were Butch, Sundance, Rosa Jordan and Johnny Latham. They were there to buy some supplies.

A week had passed since the death of Ginger Moran.

The general store and blacksmith shop were the favourite haunts of the gangs of outlaws from Hole-in-the-Wall. It could, at times, get very noisy when some of the gangs visited.

Jasper and Jesse did not look upon many of the outlaws favourably, but they accepted them as customers. Some of the more violent outlaws tried to buy the goods on the cheap, but most of them paid without too much trouble.

The sound of raised voices and curses could be heard coming from somewhere around the back of the store. There was, without doubt, an outlaw gang hanging around there, and they were having some sort of ruckus.

Johnny said with a grin, 'Sounds like someone's been sampling the contents of the saloon already.'

He was suggesting that the loud voices and curses were coming from men who had been drinking too much.

'Yeah, I guess so,' Butch grinned back at him.

Johnny said something about wanting to look around, and he and Rosa walked off in the direction of the blacksmith shop. Sundance started to follow them — he was going to check out the saloon.

'Hey, Sundie,' Butch called him back, using his pet nickname for The Kid. 'Stay out of trouble.'

Butch knew that his partner would never start any trouble, but he would not walk away from it either. If any member of the outlaw gang that was around the back of the store making all the noise decided to pick a fight with Sundance, then Butch knew that The Kid would retaliate.

Sundance turned back to him. 'You know I always avoid trouble, *amigo*,' he said with a faint grin.

Butch headed into the general store alone, and muttered to himself, 'I guess I'll buy the supplies, then.'

Jesse Sheldon, a tall, stout man in his thirties, suddenly hurried over to Butch when he saw him enter. Jesse and his brother, Jasper, were two of the many friends of Butch and Sundance.

'You hadn't better stay here too long,' Jesse said in warning to Butch. 'Abe Gannon and his gang are here; they are around the back getting drunk and having fighting contests. They've already raided the saloon.'

Jesse knew that Gannon's stepsisters, Rosa and Louisa, were staying at Bitter Creek Ranch with Butch and The Kid, and that Gannon did not approve.

Butch frowned slightly at Jesse's words. He realized that Abe Gannon would probably erupt into a violent rage if he spotted Rosa, and especially after the death of Ginger Moran that all hell would break loose. Even though Butch had a fearless nature, he always tried to avoid trouble. He knew eventually there would have to be a reckoning with Abe Gannon, but he did not think that behind the general store of Jesse and Jasper Sheldon was the place it should happen. His frown deepened as he wondered where Sundance was.

Butch turned to go out to look for his partner, but Jesse caught hold of his arm, and said in a low voice, 'That ain't all. Marshal Joe Latham was seen around here a couple of days ago asking questions about you and Sundance. He knows about the two of you taking over Bitter Creek Ranch from Nathan Casey, he knows that Johnny works for you, and he's trying to catch you ...'

US Marshal Joe Latham was the corrupt and sadistic father of young Johnny, and the man who had vowed to capture Butch and The Kid.

While heading towards the blacksmith shop with Rosa, Johnny took her hand. He was besotted with her and he hoped to start courting her; he was unaware of her secret feelings for Sundance.

Johnny led her behind the blacksmith shop where he thought they would be alone. He intended to tell her of his feelings, and to ask her if they could start courting.

Sundance was walking behind them,

and he smiled as he watched them disappear down the side and to the rear of the blacksmith shop. He had so far spent two days giving shooting lessons to Rosa, and she was learning fast, he felt a little proud of this fact. He strolled on past the blacksmith shop and into the recently erected, and for the time being, deserted saloon.

Johnny still held Rosa's hand as he pulled her to a stop. No one else seemed to be about. They could hear the cries and curses coming from the outlaw gang who were still causing an uproar behind the general store a few yards further on.

The youngsters stood on the dirt path behind the blacksmith shop and Johnny pulled Rosa closer to him. He was smiling with affection as he looked into her brown eyes.

Rosa felt uncomfortable at the smile that Johnny was giving her. She realized that he liked her, and she also liked him. She liked his cheeky smile and friendly, trusting nature, but he did not set her heart on fire the way that Sundance did.

All Johnny's attention was on Rosa, and all he could think about was what he wanted to say to her. He had not noticed that they were being watched.

Rocky Moran, a very violent and ruthless killer and cousin of the late Ginger Moran, was a member of Abe Gannon's outlaw gang. He had been loitering behind the blacksmith shop, and his eyes had started glowing with malice when he saw Rosa and Johnny suddenly appear.

Rocky Moran was tall and strongly built with a long nose and brown hair. He had ducked into cover in the passageway between the blacksmith shop and saloon when he had first seen the young couple heading his way. Peering cautiously round the side of the building, Rocky watched them.

Johnny was still looking lovingly into Rosa's eyes, and was just about to speak to her when Rocky made his move.

Before Johnny realized what was happening, Rocky sprang out quickly from around the side of the blacksmith shop and grabbed Rosa from behind. His huge right arm encircled her neck, almost choking her, and he dug his gun into her back.

Rosa could not speak because of Moran's hold on her neck and she found it hard to breathe. She clawed desperately at his arm trying to loosen his hold. She could smell Rocky's sweat and it made her feel nauseous.

Horrified, Johnny's first thought was to reach for his gun.

'Leave it,' Moran rasped, 'or she's dead!'

Moran's gun dug hard into Rosa's back.

Johnny stayed his hand; his heart was hammering wildly and he thought of calling out for Sundance or Butch.

'Don't make a sound,' Rocky warned as though reading Johnny's thoughts, 'and get your hands up high!'

Fearing for Rosa's life, Johnny raised his hands.

'Now, walk in front of me,' Rocky ordered. 'Slowly, one wrong move and I kill her.'

Johnny moved forward in front of Moran and Rosa, walking slowly.

'Now you, pretty lady,' Rocky growled to Rosa, 'stop clawing at my arm and put your hands up high where I can see them!'

Gannon had told Moran about the incident at Bitter Creek Ranch and about Rosa's hidden gun.

Trembling, but trying to remain brave, and still struggling to breathe, Rosa raised her hands high enough for Rocky to see them.

'Keep walking forwards, boy. Head towards the back of the general store, and keep your hands high,' Rocky ordered Johnny while he forced Rosa forward.

The three of them, Rocky Moran and his two captives, walked slowly towards the area behind the back of the general store where the noise of Gannon and his men was coming from, and where eventually, to Rosa's horror, they met up with Abe Gannon and the other members of his gang.

Abe Gannon and his gang were amusing themselves by having a fist-fighting contest while drinking whiskey and other spirits. Whiskey and spirits that they had plundered from the soon-to-be-opened saloon.

The rules of the contest had been made up by the outlaws themselves.

The two men who were opposing each other in the contest would first toss a coin to determine who would go first, and the man who won the toss would then throw the first punch. His opponent would have to stand perfectly still and take the blow. If the blow only felled him and failed to knock him out, then it would be his turn to throw a punch at the man who had won the toss and try to render him unconscious. They would then take turns at throwing a punch at each other until one of them was unconscious.

Gannon particularly enjoyed the contest because he usually managed to knock out most of his men with just one punch.

Although the gang had been drinking, they were actually quite sober; they were hard drinkers and used to alcohol. They intended to take a lot of the drink back to Hole-in-the-Wall.

Abe Gannon watched with a smug grin on his face as his second opponent that morning fell unconscious at his feet.

Blood poured from the nose of Walt Austin as he lay unmoving on the ground.

There were four men with Gannon that morning, and one of the men, Jimmy Kenner, threw a glass of whiskey over Austin's face.

Whiskey and blood flowed down Walt Austin's face as he started moaning.

Gannon laughed unsympathetically as he looked at the prone man. 'You next, Jimmy,' he said with relish to Kenner.

Jimmy Kenner did not look too happy at the prospect of facing Gannon in the fist-fighting contest.

One of Gannon's men, Carl Vance, who had already lost in the contest, and who was just coming round to his senses, was sitting propped up against a huge boulder. His face was blood-smeared and he looked dazed. Gannon's second opponent, Walt Austin, was still moaning on the ground.

Gannon, his right fist already bunched up, was waiting for Jimmy Kenner to toss a coin.

There were a few cuts on Gannon's face, showing that he had not always won the toss, but he had definitely won the contests.

A nervous and reluctant Kenner prepared to toss a coin. Gannon called out, 'Heads,' before Jimmy could speak.

But, as Jimmy tossed the coin, they were suddenly interrupted.

'Hey, Abe,' Rocky Moran shouted, 'look what I got for you!'

Gannon turned to look and his face showed his immense delight as he saw Rosa and Johnny.

Moran's forearm was still tight around Rosa's throat, her hands were still raised high, and Moran's gun still dug into her back.

Johnny stood sullenly in front of them with his hands raised.

Gannon crossed quickly over to them.

'Greetings, dear sister,' he snarled at Rosa, 'you'll soon be back at Hole-in-the-Wall with me!'

Rosa was almost choking in the hold of Rocky Moran, but she gave her step brother a look of hate. She still trembled, but she tried hard not to show her fear.

'You leave her alone!' Johnny cried out.

Gannon turned to the lad just as Jimmy Kenner who had just tossed the coin suddenly yelled, 'If those two youngsters are here, then it means that either Butch or Sundance must be here somewhere too!'

'Yeah.' Gannon's eyes fairly glowed with loathing at Kenner's words. He had not forgotten about Ginger's death. He felt almost certain that Sundance was to blame for the death of Ginger Moran.

'Let's just go,' Jimmy Kenner urged Gannon. 'We can take Rosa with us.' He was in no hurry to tangle with Butch and Sundance so soon after their last encounter when he had been left with a bullet injury from Sundance's gun. It had only been a slight injury, but he felt that

60

he might not be so lucky the next time.

'I ain't running away from Butch and Sundance,' Gannon almost spat out, 'and I'm not forgetting that one of them killed Ginger, and anyway, we have a hostage.' He grinned at Rosa, and said to Rocky who held her, 'Keep a tight hold of her, Rocky, not Butch or Sundance will try anything while you've got hold of her.'

Rocky grinned back at him. 'I've got her all right, she can't get away.'

He was hoping that either Butch or Sundance did try something; he wanted them to pay for the death of his cousin.

'Let's go, Abe,' Jimmy urged Gannon again. 'We have a hostage like you said, and we can maybe set up an ambush for either Butch or The Kid on the way back to Hole-in-the-Wall.'

Jimmy Kenner's words made sense to Gannon; he liked the idea of setting up an ambush for Butch or Sundance. He knew that whichever one of the partners was there at the general store, then that man would follow him to try and rescue Rosa.

Gannon grinned and nodded to Kenner, but as he looked at Johnny again his eyes suddenly glinted as the thought of a cruel action came to him. He said to Kenner, 'I just have to finish off here first … I think I have a young volunteer for the next fist-fight with me. I might even break his jaw.'

Johnny felt his stomach lurch as he caught Gannon's meaning. He had seen Gannon in action in the fist-fighting contests on one of his visits to Hole-in-the-Wall with Butch.

'What was it you shouted out to me, boy?' Gannon called out to Johnny in a harsh voice. 'It was to leave Rosa alone, wasn't it? Well, I'll make you regret trying to stand up to me.'

Gannon clenched his massive right fist once more into a ball, his knuckles cut and bleeding from his previous contests. He called Johnny over to him.

Gannon's first opponent, Carl Vance, still sat propped up groggily against the boulder and showing little interest in what was happening around him.

Gannon's second opponent, Walt Austin, got gingerly to his feet, and stood holding his bandanna against his bleeding nose.

Johnny moved unsteadily to stand facing Abe Gannon, lowered his hands, and waited in an anxious state as Gannon instructed Kenner to pick up the coin and toss it again.

Jimmy tossed the coin and as it whizzed through the air, Gannon told Johnny to call.

Johnny's voice sounded shaky as he said, 'Tails.'

The coin landed in the dirt, Kenner took a look at it, a smirk appeared on his face, and he said, 'It's heads.'

Johnny's face went pale, and he found it hard to swallow. He was not a nervous person, he was a very confident 17-year-old, but his build was only slight compared to the heavy-set build of Abe Gannon.

'That's too bad, ain't it, boy,' Gannon laughed, a loud and ghastly sound.

After Jesse Sheldon's warning, Butch quickly left the general store and went seeking his partner. He headed towards the blacksmith shop, but saw no sign of him. He then walked on towards the saloon, but he stopped as he heard Gannon's loud laugh coming from behind the store. He guessed that if there was some trouble going on, then that was where Sundance probably was.

Thinking that he would find Sundance there, Butch made his way towards the back of the general store.

Butch caught his breath sharply when he came upon the scene involving Abe Gannon and his gang. There was no sign of Sundance, but Johnny and Rosa were in big trouble. Butch had to do some quick thinking; he did not have time to walk away and look for Sundance because Gannon was about to strike Johnny. He also realized that there was probably nothing he could do to help Rosa right at that moment. He was not in a good position to even risk taking a shot at Rocky Moran, and drawing his gun might put Rosa's life in more danger, but maybe he could do something for Johnny.

A leering Gannon was preparing to smash his fist into young Johnny's face when Butch called out, 'How about trying that with me, Abe?'

All eyes turned to look at Butch. His calling out had surprised them.

Just feet in front of Butch and to his left stood Rocky Moran with his tight grip on Rosa and his gun in her back.

Although feeling scared and half-strangled, Rosa was extremely happy to see Butch.

A few yards to Butch's right was Abe Gannon and young Johnny.

Carl Vance was a bit of a distance away on the edge of the dirt path and propped against a boulder. Rocks, shrubs and tall grasses bordered the path.

Jimmy Kenner and Walt Austin were standing to the side of Gannon and Johnny, and they stepped forward closer to Butch while drawing their guns and aiming at him.

Austin's gun hand was a bit wobbly as he was still feeling the effects of being rendered unconscious by Gannon.

The situation was bad and Butch knew it. He could not call out for Sundance because of the hold that Rocky Moran had on Rosa. He knew that Moran would not hesitate to kill her.

Butch started to whistle softly, trying to make it look as though he was whistling unconcernedly while waiting for Gannon to acknowledge his challenge.

The whistle was actually a signal to The Kid. Butch knew that it was a slim chance, but he was hoping desperately that wherever his partner was, Sundance would somehow hear his signal.

Gannon turned his attention to Butch, a huge smirk on his face.

'I'll happily try it with you, Butch,' Gannon snarled, 'and then the boy!'

A shaking Johnny breathed easier, and he moved to one side as Butch took his place in front of Gannon.

Butch gave the white-faced Johnny a

confident smile.

Jimmy Kenner ordered Johnny to stand against the back of the general store and place his hands on his head.

Johnny obeyed; he was worried about Rosa and Butch and wished that there was something he could do to help them, but he did not want to risk Rosa's life.

It was a slightly groggy Walt Austin who covered Johnny with his gun while Kenner stayed close to Gannon and Butch.

Gannon's right fist was a tight ball as he smirked at Butch, who stood motionless facing him with an unconcerned look in his compelling blue eyes.

Before throwing a punch at Butch, Gannon first shot a look at Kenner who stood to the side of him.

Kenner nodded. He knew what was expected of him. He had done it before.

Gannon gave a harsh laugh and slammed his right fist hard into Butch's face, hitting him just above the right eyebrow, and at the same time, Jimmy Kenner darted forward and pulled on

Butch's arm, causing the outlaw to fall heavily to the ground.

Butch lay on his back, winded by the fall. Blood streamed from a cut above his right eyebrow, and everything was spinning round. For a moment he could not move.

Gannon gave another harsh laugh as he stood over Butch. 'You'll regret Ginger's death,' he said with malice in his voice.

Jimmy Kenner quickly straddled the supine torso of the fallen Butch. He placed each of his knees on Butch's arms, pinning them to the ground, and then he bunched up his right fist, intending to pummel the helpless outlaw.

'Hey,' Gannon snarled, moving towards the pair, 'he's mine, Jimmy!'

'Let me have him first, Abe,' Jimmy begged. 'He once stopped me from having my way with Louisa at Hole-in-the-Wall, I owe him this.'

'OK,' Gannon spoke grudgingly. He was not in the least bit bothered about Kenner almost raping his stepsister. 'But don't kill him, leave some for me, I want to be the one to kill him.'

'No!' Rocky Moran shouted out. 'Let me do that, I want to take some revenge for my cousin's death.'

Both Johnny and Rosa were aghast at what was happening, but they both knew that if Gannon and his men did kill Butch, then Sundance's way of taking revenge would be too terrifying to even think about.

Sundance wandered around the not long erected saloon. It did not have a name as yet, and a lot of the whiskey and spirit bottles were missing from behind the long, wooden panelled bar. They had been looted by Gannon and his gang.

There was a roulette wheel in the centre of the room, a piano in one corner, and some tables and chairs scattered about. Some of the tables were gaming tables.

There was a long mirror and a rather provocative picture on the wall behind the bar. A row of spittoons were spaced along the floor. There was also a flight of wooden stairs that led up to some upstairs rooms. Sundance grinned to

himself while speculating what the upstairs rooms were for.

Sundance played for a while on the
roulette wheel before leaving the saloon.

As The Kid strolled past the blacksmith
shop on his way to the general store to
join Butch, he stopped abruptly as he
thought he heard a whistling sound.

It was very faint and he could have
been mistaken, but he felt sure that he
had heard it, and he instantly felt some
alarm: it was the secret whistle between
himself and Butch.

Wherever his partner was, Sundance
sensed that he was in trouble and needed
him, but he was uncertain where to look.

Sundance cursed low, fear for Butch
passed through his mind. His uncanny
instincts told him to look behind the general store, and that was where he quickly
headed.

Moving stealthily like a panther, unseen and unheard, The Kid soon closed in
on Abe Gannon and his gang. He had not
walked down the dusty, uneven dirt path
behind the store and the other wooden

buildings, but had sneaked through the thick sagebrush and huge, jagged rocks and boulders that bordered the far side of the path.

From his vantage point hidden in the rocks, Sundance had a clear view of everything that was happening in front of him.

In just a few seconds, The Kid took in the whole scene. He saw Rosa held in the painful grip of Rocky Moran, he saw Johnny standing against the back of the store with Walt Austin holding a gun on him, and he saw Butch about to be pummelled by Jimmy Kenner. He also took note of the positions of Abe Gannon and Carl Vance.

Gannon stood near to Kenner and Butch, he was waiting with a sick eagerness to watch Kenner ram his first blow into Butch's face. Vance still sat leaning back against the boulder, he was apparently still feeling very dazed.

With all of this clear in his mind, the cool, calm Sundance Kid went into action.

The Kid was mostly worried for his

partner, but he was still able to think in his usual detached way when taking any kind of action.

Lying trapped beneath the weight of Jimmy Kenner, Butch's head started to clear. His right eyebrow was pulsating with pain, and blood was flowing into his eye, but he still managed to see Kenner's bunched-up right fist that was about to smash into his face, and he tried to think of something to do to defend himself. He was known for his astuteness, but nothing came immediately to his mind. His arms were pinned by Kenner's knees, and even if he turned his head in an effort to avoid the blow, it would not help him much. Kenner's punch would still connect with his head in some spot.

Rosa and Johnny watched in helpless dismay.

Butch tried to brace himself in some way for the blow that he knew was imminent.

The blow never connected with his face.

Instead, as Kenner's fist crashed down,

the cracking of gunfire filled the air.

Jimmy Kenner screamed in pain as a bullet drilled through his right hand and blood gushed out. He clutched his hand cursing with pain, but he stayed where he was straddling Butch. His knees still pinned Butch's arms.

'Get off my partner, Kenner,' came the cold, commanding voice of The Sundance Kid as he stepped out from behind the rocks. His smoking Colt was held firmly in his right hand and, just as only a short time ago all eyes had turned on Butch, they now turned on The Kid.

Sundance stood calmly, his gun covering them all, and giving the appearance of being in complete control of everything. From where he stood he could see all that went on.

Butch smiled on first hearing and then seeing his partner, he felt his heart cheer. The Kid had heard his whistle.

Although Moran still had his painful hold on her throat, Rosa's eyes lit up when she saw Sundance.

Rocky Moran yelled to The Kid to

drop his gun or he would kill Rosa.

Sundance coldly told him to go ahead and try it.

Moran stared with uncertainty at Sundance, wondering if he was bluffing. He did not try anything.

Abe Gannon and Walt Austin both looked at Sundance in alarm. They had not reckoned on the appearance of The Kid; they had wrongly assumed that Butch was at the general store with Rosa and Johnny only.

Enraged with the pain from his shattered and bleeding right hand, Kenner did a very foolish thing: he tried to reach for his gun with his left hand.

Without hesitation, Sundance shot him through the head, and he toppled over on to his side.

Now that his arms were free, Butch scrambled to his knees. He wiped away the blood that was flowing into his right eye, which had abated a little, and he quickly drew his Colt to aim at Abe Gannon, who had taken a rapid step towards him. He told the man to raise his hands. Gannon obeyed with a huge scowl on his face.

Sundance stepped across the dirt path closer to the group, but he stayed in a position where he could watch Carl Vance as well as the others.

Butch smiled warmly at him, and he reminded himself of how lucky he was to have a partner who never let him down.

A slight acknowledging smile touched The Kid's face, a smile that most people would not have noticed, and he asked Butch in a low voice, 'Are you all right, *amigo*?'

'I'd be a lot worse if you hadn't turned up when you did,' Butch answered as cheerily as he was able to. His right eyebrow still throbbed intensely, but the blood flow had almost stopped and was starting to congeal, and then, mindful of how close Gannon stood to him, he added almost in a whisper, 'I guess you heard my signal.'

The Kid did not hear all of Butch's words, but he was able to make them out, and he gave a quick nod, and asked rather smugly, 'What did you say about staying out of trouble?'

'Abe was gonna thump Johnny in one of his fist-fights when I got here,' Butch quickly explained. 'I offered to take Johnny's place, and they tricked me.'

Sundance turned his attention to Abe Gannon. He knew about the fist-fights that Gannon liked to have at Hole-in-the-Wall, he had seen them often enough, and although he loved challenges, he had always stayed clear of the fights because of Butch's worried appeals to him. He knew how much his partner hated him getting involved in any challenges or fights.

'You bastard!' Sundance snarled angrily to Gannon. He felt utter contempt for the man. 'Johnny is just a boy compared to you!'

Gannon grunted and shrugged; he was a callous man who did not care who he battered or killed.

Sundance was tempted to punch Gannon in the face, but he controlled his anger. He would get his chance with Gannon.

Johnny was still standing against the back of the general store. Walt Austin covered the lad with his gun, but Austin did not appear to want to try using his weapon. He did not want to be The Kid's next victim.

Sundance ordered Austin to drop his gun, which he did very hastily.

Johnny darted forward to grab Austin's firearm. He aimed it at Walt and told him to raise his hands.

Austin lifted his hands.

Gannon cursed with rage at what was happening: Butch and Sundance had caused him and his men to back down again.

Gannon looked towards where Rocky Moran stood holding Rosa, signalling with his eyes for Rocky to do something.

'What about me, Sundance?' Moran asked with an evil grin. He kept his strong forearm around Rosa's neck and his gun in her back. Her hands were still raised. 'Do you still want me to try killing her?'

'Let her go,' Sundance snapped.

Rocky sniggered. 'I don't think so. You'd

better drop your gun or I will kill her!'

'Would you rather hide behind a woman's skirts than face me?' the Kid asked coldly.

Butch suddenly felt an inner chill. Sundance was challenging Moran to a draw.

Rocky sniggered again, forcing Rosa forward a little, and said menacingly, 'Drop the gun, Sundance, or I will kill her, and then I'll kill you. I owe Ginger that much.'

Sundance said impassively, 'Your cousin tried his tricks on me as well.'

Rocky glowered at The Kid and he started to squeeze back the trigger of his gun which was still digging hard into Rosa's back.

Johnny cried out, 'No!'

'Shut up, Johnny, and stay put!' Sundance snapped at him.

Rocky carried on squeezing the trigger.

Johnny looked as though he was about to dart forward, but Butch cried out, 'No, Johnny!' He knew that his partner had something in mind.

Sundance started to lower his Colt. Rocky Moran smiled in triumph, he was sure that he held all the cards, and that he would soon be able to shoot Sundance dead.

Sundance was just on the point of letting his Colt fall from his fingers, but then, in a flickering blur of movement and in just one motion, he raised his gun and fired.

The Kid's aim was true, and the bullet whizzed over Rosa's head and straight through the forehead of the absolutely stupefied Rocky Moran.

Butch smiled in admiration at The Kid, and breathed out, 'Bravo, partner.'

Words of praise meant nothing to Sundance, but a smile flickered for a moment in his grey-blue eyes as he looked at Butch.

Moran reeled backwards for half a second with blood spurting from his forehead, and then his body seemed to crumple up and he fell dead.

Rosa started spluttering and gasping in air as the choking hold on her throat was released.

Johnny ran up to her and pulled her into his arms. He held her tenderly as she continued to gasp in air.

While still keeping his gun on Abe Gannon, Butch got to his feet.

Butch was unsteady on his feet, so Sundance went over to stand near to him in case Gannon felt like trying something.

Sundance also kept his eye on Walt Austin and Carl Vance.

Butch grinned at Gannon and said, 'Looks like your gang's getting smaller.'

Gannon glared at him with bitter hatred. He still had his hands raised and he hated being in the embarrassing position that he was in and the fact that two more of his men had died. He asked sharply, 'Can we go now?'

'Not just yet,' Sundance answered him coldly, 'your fist-fighting contest isn't over yet.'

Both Butch and Gannon caught his meaning.

Gannon grimaced; he knew that Sundance was just as tough and strong as he was, maybe even more so.

'And,' Sundance continued with just as much coldness in his voice, 'I am standing in for Johnny, and I believe that you've already had your go at throwing a punch, so now, it's my turn.'

Butch took a long, deep breath; as much as he hated violence he felt that Gannon deserved this. The man would have hit young Johnny as hard as he could and probably done the boy some serious harm. Gannon had also tricked Butch in the fist-fighting contest. Butch also felt that this was his responsibility — he was the one who had offered to stand in for Johnny originally. He was not going to leave this task to The Kid.

'No, partner,' Butch said seriously to The Kid, 'I am the one who should be standing in for Johnny, this is actually my turn ... and I am the one they were happily going to thrash to death.'

Sundance knew that Butch was tough enough to take on Gannon. His partner might not look it on the outside, but Butch had an inner toughness and he was more than capable of holding his own in a fist-fight, and just as Butch had total belief in him, then Sundance felt the same about Butch.

Sundance, however, hesitated as he looked at the blood that was congealed just above Butch's right eyebrow. Butch had already taken a hard blow from Gannon's fist.

Butch looked into The Kid's eyes. He knew what his partner was thinking and he said in a quiet voice that only Sundance heard, 'I'm OK to do this.'

A faint smile showed in Sundance's eyes. 'Go ahead,' he said softly.

Abe Gannon looked happier now that Sundance was no longer his opponent, and he relaxed a little and lowered his hands as Butch stepped up to him.

Sundance, on seeing how Gannon had suddenly relaxed, told him icily, 'You won't be looking that relaxed in a few seconds, Abe.'

Butch grinned at his partner. The Kid's faith in him meant a lot.

Gannon's remaining gang members,

Walt Austin and Carl Vance, stayed unmoving where they were. They had no intention of trying anything while Sundance was around, and while he still held his gun.

Johnny and Rosa walked up to join them. Johnny had his arm around Rosa's shoulders.

She looked a little pale, and smiled nervously at Sundance.

He said to her, 'I wouldn't have fired if I hadn't been sure of hitting him.'

She said simply, 'I know.'

Sundance did not say anything else to her. He turned back to watch Butch and Gannon.

Butch bunched up the fingers of his right hand into a tight fist.

Gannon had a smirk on his face as he watched Butch.

The smirk vanished in a flash as Butch swung his right fist and sent a crashing blow into Gannon's face.

The blow struck Gannon on the jaw, lifted him clear of the ground, and hurled him backwards to land with a heavy thud in the dirt a few feet away.

Gannon lay still, blood trickling down his jaw; he was obviously unconscious.

The Kid squeezed Butch's arm. 'Bravo, partner,' he said quietly.

3

Butch and Johnny Latham were riding through an open stretch of grassland alongside the Powder River. It was a warm, sunny day and they were riding two Quarter Horses. The animals had recently been trained by Butch and Sundance.

The horses had bucked a little at first, but were now settling down to a steady trot.

Johnny had been on a recent visit to the town of Casper, and while he was there, he had met up with Jacob Hurley, the governor of Wyoming.

Governor Hurley was a friend of young Johnny's, and he was also a friend of Butch and Sundance.

The two outlaws had friends from all walks of life and in the most unlikely places.

Johnny and Jacob Hurley had discussed

something between them. It was a discussion about something that would have a strong effect on Butch and Sundance.

Johnny started to tell Butch about the discussion. 'You know that I went to Casper last week, don't you?' Johnny began.

Butch nodded, his right eyebrow was still discoloured and slightly swollen from Gannon's punch.

'Well,' Johnny carried on, 'while I was there, I met up with Governor Jacob Hurley, I know he is your friend too, and we got talking, and Jacob mentioned something about a pardon.'

Butch suddenly looked sharply at Johnny. He was wondering where this conversation was heading, and he reined his horse to a stop. 'A pardon?' he asked, his voice was unusually sharp.

Johnny pulled his horse to a stop next to Butch. 'Yeah,' he smiled. He had not been put off at all by Butch's harsh voice. 'Jacob thinks that there might be the possibility of a pardon — '

'A pardon for me?' Butch interrupted

almost savagely. He was clearly, and very unusually for him, angry, and his voice got louder as he said, 'You can forget about that, Johnny, there's no way I'd accept a pardon unless Sundance gets one too!'

Johnny grinned. Butch's sudden angry attitude did not bother him. He understood why Butch felt like he did.

'I know that,' Johnny said with emphasis, 'and so does Jacob. Hell, everyone who knows you and Sundance knows that. Jacob thinks that he can get a pardon for both of you.'

Butch smiled, his anger vanishing as suddenly at it had begun, but he doubted that Jacob Hurley would have much luck in obtaining a pardon for himself and The Kid.

'Will you tell Sundance?' Johnny asked.

'No,' Butch said firmly as he kneed his horse back into a trot, 'and neither will you. If and when he needs to know, then I will tell him.'

Butch felt almost certain that Hurley would not be able to arrange a pardon for himself and Sundance, and he did not want to trouble Sundance with something that would probably never happen, so he put it out of his mind.

A couple of miles further on from where Butch and Johnny were riding, Sundance was riding another recently trained Quarter Horse. He rode slowly; he was keeping on the alert as Butch had told him of Jesse Sheldon's warning about Marshal Joe Latham being in the area.

The Kid rode through a narrow canyon, and he was just riding out of it when he instinctively sensed danger and looked around him. He was riding on a narrow path with tall pine trees, dense brush and scattered rocks on either side. He did not know why, but he had the acute feeling that something was going to happen. He was just in the act of drawing his gun, when the young horse that he was riding suddenly stumbled and threw The Kid forward in the saddle, sending him off balance and delaying his action in drawing his gun.

Suddenly, and from out of nowhere

it seemed, a rope swished through the air, the loop dropped over The Kid's shoulders and was pulled tight, pinning his arms to his sides, and he was jerked forcefully from the saddle.

Sundance struck the ground hard on his back and immediately two men darted out from the undergrowth and flung themselves upon him.

The Kid was slightly dazed from his impact with the ground, and his arms were pinned by the rope, but he still fought back. He kicked out and caught one man in the stomach.

Another man scurried from the undergrowth and joined the other two in trying to subdue Sundance.

The three men did not find it easy, and they received several kicks and knocks before they eventually succeeded in turning The Kid over on to his face and tying his hands securely behind his back with a long strip of rawhide.

Sundance was then hauled to his feet, and he saw who his three captors were. One of them was the ruthless US marshal, Joe Latham, the other two were his deputies, Wade Ashton and Jeb Taylor. Sundance knew all three men by sight and reputation — he and Butch had spent a lot of time in the last couple of years avoiding traps set for them by Latham and his deputies.

All three of the lawmen had cuts and marks on their faces from their scuffle with Sundance.

The rawhide around The Kid's wrists was so tight that it cut into his flesh, and his arms were still pinned by the rope that had swished through the air and pulled him out of the saddle. Joe Latham held the end of the rope.

'Hello, Sundance,' Latham drawled, tugging on the rope that was wrapped around Sundance's arms with a satisfied look on his face. He had tried several times in the past to snare Butch and Sundance, but they had always slipped through his traps.

'That was a bit of luck for us,' Latham sneered at The Kid, 'your horse stumbling like that, but not so lucky for you.'

Joe Latham was a tall man, about six foot three inches in height. His body was sturdy and solid. He was powerfully built with fair hair and hardened features.

Sundance did not say anything, his cold eyes just looked impassively at the three men.

'Is your partner around here somewhere?' Latham demanded.

The marshal had not noticed anyone else riding nearby when he had first spotted Sundance, but that did not mean that Butch was not in the area. He knew that the outlaws rarely strayed far from each other. Still Sundance kept quiet.

Latham scowled with sudden anger as he realized that Sundance would never answer him regarding Butch. He had heard of the partners' loyalty to each other. He turned to his deputies and pointed to the trail through the canyon to the left of him where they had first spotted Sundance and said, 'Ride back down the trail for a little way, see if Butch Cassidy is around somewhere, and if he is bring him back here.'

Taylor and Ashton quickly mounted their horses and rode off.

Latham turned his hard grey eyes on to Sundance and said, 'You know that I usually hang my prisoners on the spot, don't you? That's the reason that you are tied up with rawhide and not shackled with the handcuffs. We are not taking you in, we are going to hang you.'

The Kid just looked unemotionally into Latham's cold eyes. He knew that the callous marshal enjoyed hanging his prisoners instead of taking them to stand trial.

'Most of my prisoners either start blubbing or begging for their lives,' Latham grinned at The Kid. 'Which will you do?'

Latham's only answer was the same emotionless stare, which was starting to irritate him. He wanted to force some emotion into those expressionless eyes.

Sundance would never let Latham's gloating bother him and he would never show any emotion. The only regret he felt was for Butch and the ranch. He knew how completely devastated and disconsolate Butch would be by his death.

Butch and Johnny were still riding through the grassland beside the Powder River when Johnny said, 'Can we ride back to the ranch now? I promised Rosa that I'd take her out on a picnic today.'

Butch smiled; he knew that Johnny was sweet on Rosa, but he also knew that the girl was strongly attracted to Sundance. Even as a 13-year-old at Hole-in-the-Wall, she had followed Sundance around almost everywhere.

'You ride back, Johnny,' Butch said, 'and take Rosa on her picnic, I'll go catch Sundance up. I want to ride a few more miles on this horse.' Butch enjoyed riding miles while training the horses. He and The Kid often raced each other through the grassland.

Johnny wheeled his horse round and urged him into a quick pace back to the ranch.

Butch trotted along slowly on the Quarter Horse. He knew that he had plenty of time to catch Sundance up. He spoke to the horse and patted it encouragingly. He loved horses and had a way with them, similar to the way he had with people. The path he was riding along became narrower and the grassland gave way to more rugged terrain; tall trees and huge rock piles appeared on each side of the trail.

Butch nudged his horse with his heels and the animal speeded up into a canter towards the mouth of a canyon a few yards ahead. He was unaware that he was being watched.

Deputies Jeb Taylor and Wade Ashton were hiding among the huge rock piles at the mouth of the canyon. They grinned with evil delight when they saw Butch.

Jeb Taylor was dark-haired and brawny. Wade Ashton was blond-haired and thin.

As Butch cantered along he was being watchful, he knew that he could not afford to be too relaxed with Marshal Joe Latham in the area, but what happened next was something that he had not anticipated.

Butch was caught completely off guard as, just like what had happened to

Sundance, there was the sudden swishing of a rope, the loop dropped over his shoulders, pinning his arms, and he was yanked from the saddle.

Butch landed heavily on his side, and before he could even attempt to move, Taylor and Ashton sprang out from the cover of the rocks and flung themselves upon him.

After a brief struggle, Butch was turned over on to his face, and his wrists were tied tightly behind his back with rawhide.

Feeling breathless and sore, Butch was pulled to his feet. He recognized Latham's deputies immediately.

Butch thought about his partner with sadness as he considered what was in store for him. He knew that the ruthless Latham would most likely hang him.

The lariat was still wrapped around Butch's arms, and Jeb Taylor tightened the lariat securely and held on to the end of the rope.

'Marshal Latham will be very pleased to see you, Cassidy,' Taylor grinned.

'Yeah,' Ashton agreed with a short

laugh. 'We'll have a double hanging.'

Butch almost passed out in shock when he heard those words. It could only mean that they had caught Sundance as well as himself.

Taylor confirmed Butch's fears when he said, 'We have your partner too; he's just through the canyon with Marshal Latham.'

Butch felt fear suddenly clutch at his heart. It was not the thought of being hanged that frightened him, it was the thought of having to watch Sundance hang — that was something he could not bear to think about, and he at once started to think of a way out of this seemingly hopeless situation for himself and The Kid.

Taylor and Ashton swung up on their horses and Butch was made to walk in front of them while Taylor held on to the end of the lariat.

Joe Latham saw them first. They were coming out from the canyon, his two deputies and their captive. He could not hide his elation when he saw Butch walking in front with his hands tied behind him.

'Well,' Latham beamed at Sundance, 'look who's coming to join us.'

The Kid's heart sank when he saw his partner. He felt fearful of what they might do to Butch, but it never would show, not in his eyes, his face, or in any part of him.

Taylor and Ashton got down from their horses and dragged Butch forward to stand opposite The Kid.

Butch glanced sadly at his partner and saw a flash of reassurance in Sundance's eyes.

Taylor let go of the end of the lariat and it dangled from Butch's arms, but Latham held on to the end of the rope that was wrapped around Sundance's arms.

'I've waited a long time for this moment.' Latham still beamed with elation.

'What a sad life you must have, Latham,' Sundance said to him, and he said it with such icy calmness that Latham's beaming smile of pure delight instantly vanished.

Butch lowered his head to hide his

smile. In spite of their very grave situation, Sundance could still make him smile.

Latham's eyes were wild with fury as he cried out to Sundance, 'You'll not sound so calm when you watch us hang your partner!'

'Think so?' Sundance asked him with the same icy calmness.

Latham's words had chilled Sundance to the bone. He knew that watching them hang Butch would hurt him like nothing else ever could, but he would never let them see it.

Latham swore and then smirked and said chillingly, 'We'll soon be putting that to the test.'

The marshal was furious at the calm demeanour of both outlaws. It was something that he had not experienced before from men whom he had been about to hang. He was used to his prisoners showing some fear or begging for their lives.

Butch still smiled as he kept his glance downwards.

Latham angrily reached out to take

the outlaws' guns from their holsters. He threw them into the dirt. 'You can look at your guns lying there as you hang,' he smirked.

He did not bother to search the outlaws for any hidden weapons. He believed that they were helpless and could not escape their grisly fate.

Latham then looked purposely from Butch to Sundance. 'Who shall I hang first?' he asked.

He was hoping to see some spark of emotion between them.

No emotion was in Sundance's eyes, and Butch looked firmly downwards.

Jeb Taylor suddenly spoke up, saying, 'We got Curt and Mick coming to join us soon. Shouldn't we wait for them to get here before we hang these two?'

Curt and Mick were two more of Latham's deputies.

'No!' Latham fairly screamed. 'Let's get on with this hanging.'

The marshal then looked at Butch with a malevolent glint in his eyes. He appeared to have made up his mind on who he would hang first.

Sundance felt his heart turn to ice. They were going to hang Butch in front of him, and for him, that was far worse than being hanged himself. He tried to think of some action he could take, and as he was thinking, Butch suddenly lifted his head and looked into his partner's eyes. An unspoken message of understanding passed between them and Butch got ready to put on the act of his life.

Holding on tightly to the end of the lariat that was wrapped around Sundance's arms, Latham said with eagerness to his deputies who stood on either side of Butch, 'We'll hang Cassidy first.'

He looked towards a row of tall trees on the edge of the trail. 'One of those trees will do,' he remarked, the eagerness still in his voice.

Jeb Taylor grabbed hold of Butch's arm and held him in a tight grip as Ashton fetched his own horse over to stand underneath a wide branch of one of the tall trees. Taylor and Ashton together started to drag Butch over to the horse.

In front of the startled eyes of Latham and his deputies, Butch suddenly started to writhe in the grip of Taylor and Ashton, and he screamed out, 'No, no, I don't want to hang!'

Butch's struggles became more fierce as the deputies tried to hold on to him, he pulled backwards almost pulling the deputies over. His eyes were filled with terror.

'No, no!' he shrieked.

Latham was staring at Butch in bewilderment. He was used to his victims showing fear, but he was quite taken aback by Butch's actions as Butch had previously shown none. He knew about Butch's reputation as a smart thinker, and it crossed his mind that Butch might be faking it all.

The marshal glanced slyly at Sundance; he wanted to see The Kid's reaction to Butch's behaviour. All he saw in Sundance's eyes was disgust and anger.

'Coward!' The Kid spat at his partner.

Taylor and Ashton were still trying to drag Butch forward as he thrashed about in their hold.

Butch then started to blubber. 'No, don't hang me!' he wailed.

'So, I guess you want Sundance to hang first,' Latham stated. He felt very sceptical about how Butch was reacting to the hanging, and was trying to find out for certain if Butch was feigning.

'Go ahead and hang him,' Butch begged, 'but please, don't hang me!' He still writhed in the grip of Taylor and Ashton, tears streaming down his face as he struggled. 'Hang him, but don't hang me!'

'You snivelling coward!' Sundance yelled at him, and then he added a few swear words.

Joe Latham was still not fully convinced. He said to Butch with a sneer, 'You don't mean that, you've been Sundance's partner for a long time and you think a lot of him.'

'No!' Butch cried hoarsely. 'I don't, I just use him!'

Latham looked undecided for a moment.

'I use him!' Butch wailed on. 'He's good with a gun and he protects me!'

Sundance snorted angrily.

'Everyone knows you two are close,' Latham pointed out, looking keenly from Butch to Sundance. 'I'm not buying this, you are just delaying the hanging.'

Butch still continued to struggle desperately as Taylor and Ashton held on to his arms. 'It's all an act on my part!' he cried out. 'I make use of his gun, why else would I put up with such a dreary, stupid and obnoxious person like him?'

Sundance suddenly sprang forward and spat in Butch's face.

Butch struck out with his right leg, kicking Sundance full in the stomach, sending him hurtling back past where the horse stood beside the edge of the trail and into the cover of the dense trees and sagebrush.

The end of the lariat that Latham had been holding was torn from his grasp, and the marshal at once drew his gun and spun round to go after The Kid. He fired a shot wildly into the trees. He did not want either of the outlaws to get away.

Butch was desperate to stop Latham from shooting Sundance, and even as the two deputies tried to hold on to him, he kicked out again, and his kick struck the back of Latham's right leg. The marshal yelled out in pain, fell down into the dirt, and dropped his gun.

Latham was back up on his feet quickly and picked up his gun; his face was red with anger.

Butch, meanwhile, was thrashing about and kicking out with as much effort as he could manage as Taylor and Ashton tried to restrain him. He was doing all this to keep their attention on him, and not on Sundance; he was trying to give his partner the precious seconds that he needed to free himself. Butch knew that Sundance had a knife and a small derringer hidden in his boots.

Latham cursed. 'You bastard, Cassidy!' he screamed at Butch. 'I knew you were faking!'

The marshal then ordered his deputies to go and find Sundance.

Taylor and Ashton let go of the struggling Butch, and Latham struck the outlaw hard on the side of the face.

Butch fell to the ground. He landed on his right side with a thud and a groan. Blood streaked down the side of his face from a wide cut that had opened up from Latham's punch. Latham stood over him, then stooped lower and aimed his gun at Butch's chest. 'Stay still!' he snapped.

Latham then yelled into the trees, 'Sundance, you get back here or I'll kill your partner!'

Butch, when he had got his breath back and with a mischievous twinkle in his eyes, said, 'You're gonna hang us anyway, ain't you, Marshal?'

Latham swore, and drawing back his foot he kicked Butch several times in the ribs. Butch gasped in pain.

The marshal could have kicked Butch until his ribs broke or until he was dead, but he did not; he wanted the outlaw to suffer most when he was choked to death at the end of a rope.

'You are lucky that I want to hang you so badly,' Latham rasped at Butch, 'or I'd shoot you dead right now, or kick you to death.'

Lying on his stomach behind a tree, Sundance knew that he only had seconds to act, and ignoring the sore feeling in his stomach from Butch's kick, he got quickly to his knees, and with his tightly bound and throbbing hands he jerked up the pants of his right leg. His fingers felt stiff and painful as he pulled a small, folded pocket knife from out of his boot. Disregarding the pain and stiffness of his fingers, he flicked open the knife and sliced through the rawhide around his wrists, and then through the lariat pinning his arms.

When he was finally free of all the restraints, he pulled a small derringer from out of his left boot.

Latham's yell about killing Butch then reached Sundance's ears and he felt a momentary stab of alarm. He placed the folded knife down his waistband and got speedily off his knees. He heard the sound of leaves rustling to the right of him and headed that way.

With their guns drawn, Jeb Taylor and Wade Ashton prowled through the dense undergrowth and trees looking for Sundance.

They instantly froze when they heard his harsh voice behind them call out, 'Hold it, I have a gun aimed at you two.'

Taylor and Ashton looked at each other in surprise. Had The Kid really got a gun?

'Drop your guns,' Sundance called out behind them again, 'and put your hands on your heads.'

The Kid was behind them, so the deputies could not see the small derringer that he held. They hesitated.

Blond-haired Wade Ashton whispered to Taylor, 'Has he really got a gun?'

There was the unmistakeable clicking sound as Sundance squeezed back the trigger on the derringer. On hearing that sound, the two deputies dropped their guns and placed their hands on top of their wide-brimmed hats.

Sundance stepped forward to pick

up one of the dropped guns. He held the weapon firmly in his right hand and dropped the derringer back down his boot.

'Now, start walking,' Sundance ordered the two men sharply, 'we're going back to your boss.'

Butch was lying on the ground on his side gasping from the kicking and with Latham's gun aimed at his chest when Taylor and Ashton emerged from the undergrowth with their hands clasped firmly on top of their Stetsons.

Sundance's cold voice sounded behind them. 'I'm coming back, Latham!'

The left side of Butch's face was still bleeding slightly from where Latham had struck him, and his ribs throbbed with pain, but he smiled when he heard his partner's voice. He knew then that Sundance was all right.

Seconds later The Kid appeared behind the two lawmen, and ordered them to kneel down.

Butch's smile grew wider when he saw his partner.

Taylor and Ashton dropped to their knees in front of Sundance.

Latham stood not too far away from them on the narrow path covering Butch with his gun, and he stared at The Kid with fury in his eyes.

'Drop your gun, Latham!' Sundance snapped.

The marshal still aimed at Butch, and he replied coolly, 'You drop yours or I'll kill your partner.'

'Go ahead,' Sundance said with no emotion in his voice. 'Why should I care about someone as dreary, stupid, and obnoxious as him?'

In spite of the pain in his ribs, Butch gave a low chuckle when he heard those words. 'Sorry about that, partner!' he called.

The Kid only grunted in reply to him, then he told Latham again to drop his gun.

Instead the marshal started pulling back the trigger on his gun while aiming at Butch's chest. He was deliberately testing The Kid's nerve, and his speed and skill with a gun.

Butch knew what Latham was up to and he said mildly, 'I wouldn't do that, Marshal.'

Latham ignored him and continued to ease back the trigger.

Sundance instantly opened fire, but he did not shoot to kill. Latham was a United States marshal, and he did not want the marshal's death to be pinned on himself and Butch.

The bullet skimmed across Latham's wrist leaving a slight wound. Blood began to drip from the wound, but it was not much. Latham dropped his gun and rubbed his wrist, which hurt a lot despite the small wound.

'You shouldn't push my partner, Marshal,' Butch grinned at Latham.

'Damn you!' Latham cried out at both outlaws.

He was furious at being denied his hanging.

'Put your hands on your head, Latham,' Sundance said harshly. 'Move over by your deputies and get on your knees or

I'll kill you.'

The Kid meant it. He did not want to kill a United States marshal, but he would if he had to.

Latham could tell that Sundance was not bluffing, and he resentfully obeyed. He placed both hands on his head, his wrist still hurting and bleeding. He walked across to join his deputies and got down on his knees beside them. He glared with anger and hatred at Butch and Sundance.

With the three lawmen on their knees in front of him, The Kid called to his partner. 'Butch!' he snapped 'Get up, and get over here!'

'Oh, yes sir,' Butch said with fake humbleness.

It was difficult for Butch to get to his feet. His hands were still tied behind his back and the lariat was still wrapped around his arms, and his ribs were throbbing. He tried a few times to stand up and failed.

He was about to try again when Sundance sighed with impatience and, keeping his gun trained on Latham and his deputies, he walked the few feet between them over to Butch and pulled him to his feet with his left hand. His right hand holding the Colt never wavered.

Butch had to suppress the cry of pain from his throbbing ribs as he was pulled to his feet. He did not want Sundance to know about the kicking yet. He was worried about what The Kid might do to Latham, and he did not want any more violence.

The Kid then used his left hand to pull the pocket knife from out of his waistband. He flicked it open and cut through the rawhide that bound Butch's wrists. He handed the knife to Butch so that his partner could cut the lariat binding his arms.

Butch's fingers were numb from the tightness of the rawhide and he almost dropped the knife, but he managed to hold on to it, and after rubbing some feeling back into his fingers, he quickly slashed the rope pinning his arms.

Once free of the ropes, Butch picked up his own and Sundance's gun from out of the dirt where Latham had thrown them. He almost cried out with the pain the action caused to his ribs, and he had to stand still for a second as the pain abated.

Sundance asked him if he was all right.

The Kid had of course seen the fresh cut on Butch's face and he guessed that Latham must have hit his partner, which was why Butch was on the ground. He did not like what Latham had done, but he had let it pass.

Butch smiled quickly, trying to mask his pain. He gingerly touched the cut on his face. 'I just felt dizzy for a moment, that's all.'

Sundance stared at him. He was not satisfied with Butch's answer, and he wondered if maybe the cut was hurting more than Butch wanted to admit, but it was clear to him that Butch did not want to say anything else about it, so Sundance turned his attention to Latham and the other two lawmen.

Sundance instructed Latham and his deputies to stand up. He held his gun on them while Butch took their handcuffs from out of their belts and handcuffed their hands behind their backs.

The outlaws then used the lawmen's own lariats to tie them to the trunks of the tall trees beside the trail.

'Are you just gonna leave us here like this?' Latham snarled.

Butch remembered what Jeb Taylor had said about Curt and Mick coming to join them, and he said, 'You got some more deputies coming to join you soon, ain't you? They can release you.'

'This isn't over,' Latham vowed, 'I'll get you both one day!'

Sundance frowned at Latham's vow. He knew that the only way to stop Latham from coming after himself and Butch again was to kill him, but that was something that he could not do unless he had no other choice.

The Kid's horse had stayed close by, so they were able to catch him easily.

They decided to walk through the canyon with the horse, and then try whistling for the young Quarter Horse that Butch had been riding.

As the outlaws walked through the canyon, Butch started to feel guilty about what he had said to Latham regarding his partner, and he wondered if he had gone too far in the act that he had put on.

Butch said seriously, 'You do know, Sundie, don't you, that I never meant a word of what I said to Latham about you.'

Sundance grinned. It was typical of his warm-hearted partner to worry about something like that. Something that Sundance obviously already knew. 'Don't be stupid, *amigo*,' he said, 'of course I know that.'

He knew that Butch would die for him without any hesitation, and he would willingly die for his partner.

Butch smiled at The Kid and said, 'I'm sorry about the words I used, and I'm sorry for kicking you.'

The Kid grinned again. 'What kick?' he asked, and then he added, 'And I'm sorry for calling you a coward and swearing at you, and for spitting in your face.'

'That went right in my eye,' Butch

laughed and The Kid laughed with him.

The laughing caused Butch's ribs to start throbbing again.

They had reached the end of the canyon and were walking through the grassland beside the river when Butch whistled for the horse. The young animal came trotting up to him.

Butch start to stroke the horse's neck, but then he gasped as he felt excruciating throbs of pain from his ribs. The pain took his breath away and he started to keel over.

Sundance grabbed hold of him to keep him on his feet.

They sat down on the river-bank until Butch could breathe properly, and The Kid asked Butch sharply where he was hurt.

When Butch had recovered his breath, he told Sundance about the kicking that Latham had given him.

'You should have told me before!' Sundance yelled angrily.

He knew why Butch had not told him. It was because his partner had wanted to avoid more trouble with Latham. The Kid had managed to overlook the fact that Latham had hit Butch while he was tied up, but he would not have overlooked the kicking.

Butch knew that Sundance would probably have given Latham a severe beating.

Deep inside of Sundance (as Butch knew well) was a very vicious streak, but The Kid would have to be pushed a long way before he would ever show it.

Sundance cursed under his breath; he was angry at Latham, and angry that Butch had not told him that he was in pain, but he did not want to show too much of his anger to Butch, because he knew that surprisingly, Butch Cassidy, the smart and fearless leader of one of the most successful outlaw gangs in the West, had a sensitive side. He could be badly hurt by harsh, angry words from people whom he cared about.

The left side of Butch's face was still bleeding and Sundance went down the bank to the river to dip his bandanna in the water, then he went back to Butch and started to clean up the cut on the side of Butch's face. Butch's right eyebrow was still slightly swollen and bruised from Abe Gannon's punch.

Sundance sighed and said, 'You're gonna have to try and stay out of trouble, partner, or there'll be no room left on your face for another bruise.'

Butch started to laugh, but then caught his breath as the laughing hurt his ribs.

The Kid asked him if he could ride. Butch nodded, and they mounted their horses. Sundance helped him up on to his horse before climbing into the saddle of his own mount.

Butch said rather unhappily, 'Latham won't be satisfied until he has got us, will he?'

'No, *amigo*,' Sundance said quietly, 'he will not, which means that we'll have to be very careful.'

Later that evening, around sundown, Butch strode out on to the wooden porch of the ranch house. During the warm summer months as it was now, both he and

Sundance slept outdoors on the porch.

Hank had checked over Butch's ribs; they were badly bruised, but luckily not broken. Butch sat down in one of the rocking chairs, the pain in his ribs having lessened into just a dull ache. He set the chair in motion and started to think about Amy Bassett.

Amy and her family had been the closest neighbours to his own family when he had lived in Circleville, Utah, and he could not remember a time when he had not loved her. He knew that Amy now had another man whom she lived with.

He looked round on hearing light footsteps, and smiled as Louisa joined him. She liked joining him when he sat out on the porch. She sat down in the other rocking chair close to him.

'Are you all right?' Louisa asked him. Everyone on the ranch had heard about how Joe Latham had tried to hang Butch and Sundance.

Butch smiled as he looked into Louisa's anxious blue eyes. 'I'll live,' he replied lightly as he stopped the motion of the rocking chair.

'Johnny feels really upset about what happened to you and Sundance,' Louisa said. 'Joe Latham is his father after all.'

Butch still smiled. 'It's not Johnny's fault who his father is.'

They were silent for a moment or two, then Louisa said, 'You were lucky to escape.'

'Yeah.' Butch gave a cheeky grin. 'Lucky that Sundance had that knife and gun in his boots, and that he has a cool head.'

There was silence between them again, and then Louisa asked, 'Will you stay on the ranch and run it, or will you go back to being outlaws?'

'We are outlaws,' Butch told her, 'and at the moment we like ranching. Maybe after a few years we'll feel differently, but for now, we like what we are doing.'

Louisa really cared about him and she was not sure if she should ask him what she wanted to ask next, so she said quietly, 'Can I ask you something?'

'Sure,' he smiled.

'Would you one day like to settle down and have a wife and family?'

Her words were like a knife slicing through him, and for a moment he could not answer. He had walked out on the best woman that he had ever known.

Louisa saw his face change and she regretted her question.

'Is that what you want?' Butch eventually asked her.

'Yes, it is.'

He turned to look at her and said gently, but meaningfully, 'If that's what you want for your future, Louisa, then go and look for it. Don't waste your life staying here.'

His words saddened her.

Butch saw that and sighed. He had not wanted to upset her.

'You are very attractive, Louisa,' he told her, 'and you are a good person. The future that you want is out there somewhere, but it's not with me.'

Butch knew that she liked him, and he also knew what she had been trying to ask. In her own way, Louisa was asking him how he felt about her.

Butch reached over to her and took hold of one of her hands. He said quietly, 'I had the chance to settle down at one time and with a good woman, but it was not enough for me, I wanted something more, and a lot of people got hurt when I walked away from it … I can't go through that again.'

'But this time might be different.' Louisa looked longingly into his eyes.

For a moment, Butch felt very attracted to her, he felt quite mesmerized by her beauty and he almost started to kiss her passionately, but he managed to resist her, and said, 'There is a restless spirit inside of me, Louisa. This restless spirit drives me on, and a life of settling down with a wife and family is not the life I want.'

Louisa got up out of the rocking chair and walked away with tears clouding her eyes.

Memories of Amy started to fill Butch's mind again as he set the chair in motion.

He had loved her from the age of seven,

and he had believed that he would stay with her for as long as he lived, but then his restless spirit had emerged. He had yearned for the excitement and adventure that Amy could not give him. He had got involved with a gang of rustlers and had left her and his family.

He felt tears come to his eyes.

'Hey.' The Kid's voice broke into his sad thoughts.

Sundance had heard some of the conversation between Butch and Louisa. He had not meant to eavesdrop, he had just stepped out on to the porch looking for his partner. He had a bottle of whiskey in his hands and two glasses.

He walked over to Butch and asked, 'Do you want some company?'

The Kid wondered if Butch wanted to be alone. He knew that Butch often had moments of overwhelming guilt regarding his family. He always tried to turn Butch's mind away from his guilt, but he realized that, at times, Butch needed to be alone.

Butch stopped the rocker and took one of the glasses from The Kid and told him to fill it.

After having a drink of the whiskey, Butch gave his partner a warm smile and said, 'I don't mind your company.'

He knew that Sundance understood him. The Kid had the same restless spirit as Butch and would never judge him for leaving Amy and his family.

4

It was the middle of the afternoon and nearly three weeks since Marshal Joe Latham had tried to hang Butch and Sundance. Rosa and Louisa were cleaning out the bunkhouse when they started to discuss their futures. They were wondering if it was perhaps time to leave the ranch. They had other relatives in the town of Casper.

Rosa's long dark auburn hair was tied back with a brown silk ribbon while Louisa's long and wavy dark blond hair flowed around her shoulders.

Rosa was dressed in a lilac shirt and brown pants while Louisa wore a grey blouse and a blue riding skirt.

Rosa did not want to leave Sundance, but she knew that the outlaw would never love her the way that she wanted. Sundance seemed to like a different girl every month. He had been more courteous to her since giving her training in how to handle a gun, but that was the only difference in the way that he treated her.

Louisa did not want to leave Butch either, but she was aware that there was no future for her with him, and whenever Butch felt like being with a woman, then it was never her that he chose. He would ride to one of the neighbouring ranches where he had female friends or into Casper where he also had several lady friends.

As they sadly discussed their options, a noise from the bunkhouse door caused them to turn round.

'Hey, ladies,' Butch called to them from the doorway, 'wanna come for a ride?'

He was asking them if they wanted to exercise the horses with him.

They nodded eagerly.

Sundance was not at the ranch. He had left roughly two hours earlier to take some of the trained horses to the nearby Hemming ranch.

Johnny, who was always eager to spend some time with Rosa asked if he could go with them, and the four of them all went to the corral and saddled up four of the young Quarter Horses.

They rode for about five miles through the grassland alongside the river, where they brought the horses to a halt. They dismounted and took the animals down to the river to drink. The horses drank from the water as Butch, Johnny, Rosa, and Louisa sat down on the low river-bank.

They did not know that Abe Gannon, along with Carl Vance and Walt Austin had been watching them from the cover of some dense trees and bushes on a small ridge to the far side of the grassland.

Abe and his men had been riding back to Hole-in-the-Wall after getting some supplies from the general store of Jasper and Jesse Sheldon and while riding along on the ridge they had spotted Butch, Johnny and the girls riding through the grassland, and had seen them stop by the river to let the horses drink.

Gannon wanted revenge on Butch and Sundance. His resentment and loathing of them had been growing by the day. He was incensed at both of them for giving refuge to Rosa and Louisa, and he felt humiliated at how Butch had knocked him out with just one punch. He was also determined to somehow force Rosa and Louisa to go back with him to Hole-in-the-Wall. In his deranged mind he saw them as his property, and their job, he reasoned was to look after him and do his bidding. His face twisted into an evil grin and his eyes glowed as he looked down from the ridge at Butch, Johnny and the two girls. He turned to his two men and said, 'Let's go get them.'

Gannon, Austin and Vance rode down from the ridge and into the grassland. They rode wide through the long grass keeping out of sight of Butch and the others and when they were still a distance away, they dismounted and led their horses the rest of the way through the grassland. They tied the horses up in some trees lining the river-bank and, keeping in the cover of the trees, they crept along slowly towards Butch and his friends.

Gannon stopped once to say to his men, 'We'll take Rosa and Louisa back with us. We can kill the boy, but not Cassidy; we'll take him with us and use him to trap Sundance.'

Johnny tried to sit close to Rosa on the bank, but she sat over by Butch and started to talk to him about Sundance. She was curious about The Kid's past, but Butch told her that anything she wanted to know about Sundance she would have to ask The Kid herself. He did not like talking about his partner when he was not there, and he certainly would never tell her anything about Sundance's past. After saying that to Rosa, Butch stood up and went down the bank to the water's edge where the horses were drinking.

Rosa sighed. She should have expected an answer like that. Butch and Sundance had an incredible loyalty to each other.

Johnny moved over to sit next to her while Louisa stood up to go and join Butch at the water's edge.

Rosa and Johnny were quietly talking

together and Louisa had just got to her feet when Gannon and his men suddenly sprang out from the trees with their guns drawn.

'Don't anyone move!' Gannon snapped.

He grinned chillingly at Butch, and then at Rosa and Louisa.

Walt Austin had his gun aimed at Butch and the outlaw could do nothing but stand still.

Gannon and Vance held their guns on Rosa, Johnny, and Louisa.

'I'm taking you two back with me,' Gannon snarled to the two girls.

Louisa stood rooted to the spot in fear.

Rosa gave a gasp and got to her feet. Johnny stood up with her.

Butch thought about making a move for his gun, but then Gannon told them all to raise their hands.

Butch, Johnny, and Louisa obeyed him, but instead of raising her hands, Rosa pulled out the gun that was hidden in her waistband, and aimed shakily at her stepbrother.

Gannon laughed when he saw the gun.

He believed that she was still a useless shot. He did not know about her shooting lessons with Sundance, and he began moving towards her.

'Stay back!' Rosa cried. 'I'm not going anywhere with you!'

Still laughing, Gannon got nearer to her. Rosa pulled the trigger.

The bullet hit her stepbrother in the stomach and he sagged for a moment with his hands pressed to his injury as blood started to gush through his fingers. He had been badly injured and he dropped his gun, and fell back against Carl Vance, who lowered him to the ground with one hand.

Gannon lay in the dirt clutching his stomach and moaning. Blood was now pouring from his bullet wound.

Rosa stood holding the gun and shaking. She felt full of revulsion for what she had done.

Butch and Johnny quickly drew their guns and opened fire.

Austin and Vance began to back up quickly into the trees for cover, firing as they went.

Butch yelled to Louisa to get down as the shooting started, and Johnny pushed Rosa to the ground while ducking down himself.

Louisa was still standing rooted with fear as bullets filled the air.

Butch shouted to her again to get down and began to rush up the bank towards her.

Austin and Vance fired a few shots, but missed their targets. They both got hit themselves before they could reach the cover of the trees and mostly by Johnny's bullets as Butch was racing up the bank to Louisa.

Walt Austin suddenly made a strangled sound and his face contorted with pain as bullets struck him in the body and throat. He dropped to his knees and pitched forward on to his face.

Carl Vance got hit twice in the chest. He seemed to stagger forward a step or two and then fell headlong into the dirt. His gun exploded as he fell and the bullet struck Butch, who had run to the top of the bank and was about to push Louisa down. The bullet grazed Butch's ribs and he fell back down the low bank.

Louisa cried out as she saw Butch fall, but she could not move her legs to go to him.

Johnny was trying to comfort Rosa as he knelt beside her. She was trembling uncontrollably and would not let go of her gun. Johnny tried to prise the gun out of her hands.

Abe Gannon, meanwhile, was still moaning on the ground and holding his stomach. The blood continued to pour from his wound. Both Rosa and Louisa looked at him in horror. Louisa started to sob where she stood. Rosa was numb with shock as Johnny finally prised the gun from her hands.

Johnny wanted to go and check on Butch, but he did not want to leave Rosa and was unsure what to do. Both Rosa and Louisa were clearly traumatized.

Johnny did not have to worry about what to do for too long as another rider was fast approaching them.

The rider was Sundance. He was riding back from delivering the horses to the Hemming ranch, and as Johnny still knelt beside Rosa, Sundance swung down from his horse and raced towards them.

Sundance's heart did a somersault of fear as he spotted Butch lying at the bottom of the bank and he started to run to him.

Although badly wounded, Abe Gannon was still a dangerous threat. He somehow managed to recover enough to grab hold of his gun which lay near to him and to stand up almost straight. Gannon's eyes were glazing over as he tried to aim his gun.

A bullet struck Gannon before he could open fire.

It had been fired swiftly from Sundance's Colt as he ran to Butch. The bullet hit Gannon in the heart killing him straight away. Blood gushed out of the wound. He teetered for a second, then his body buckled, and he crashed down into the dirt on his face.

Sundance reached Butch's side.

His partner's eyes were closed and his chest was bleeding. His shirt had been ripped open by the grazing of the bullet. Sundance began to examine the wound. He was worried about how bad it might be, but he tried to hide his worry. He started to relax when he saw that Butch's injury was not too deep. It was mainly a long graze across his ribs and there was no bullet in there.

The wound was bleeding badly, though, and Sundance strapped it up using his bandanna and strips of material from Butch's already torn shirt.

Butch moaned and opened his eyes. He looked up at Sundance in surprise. 'Hey, partner,' he said in a weak voice, 'where did you spring from?'

Sundance said with a grin, 'What did I say to you about trying to stay out of trouble?'

Butch tried to grin back. 'Trouble just follows me around,' he murmured.

Back at the ranch house, Butch's wound was properly cleaned and dressed by

Hank, and then Butch was helped to his bedroom upstairs by Sundance and ordered to rest.

Butch and Sundance had a bedroom each, and Hank had the third bedroom, but while Rosa and Louisa had been staying at the ranch house, the girls had been sleeping in the bedrooms while Butch and Sundance slept outside on the porch. Johnny and the other ranch-hands slept in the bunkhouse.

Rosa and Louisa sat with Butch for a while, and then left the room.

He was starting to drift off to sleep when Sundance entered the room, and said to him in a tone that dared Butch to defy him, 'You'll stay in that bed for at least a week. Try to move out of it, and I'll tie you in it, do you understand?'

Because of his weakened state, Butch could only manage a shaky grin as he murmured, 'Oh, yes sir.'

Butch closed his eyes and drifted off to sleep. Sundance stayed with him all that night to make sure that his chest wound did not start bleeding again. He slept in a chair next to the bed.

After a week, Butch was out of the bed, but it was two weeks before Sundance would let him do anything on the ranch, and then it was only light jobs.

At the end of the second week, Butch was feeling bored and he took a stroll around the ranch buildings.

He went into the bunkhouse where he found Johnny. The lad brewed up some coffee on the pot-bellied stove and handed Butch a cup.

They sat down at the small wooden table.

Johnny sounded excited as he said, 'I've been hoping that I'd get a chance to talk to you, Butch. Do you remember that we talked about Jacob Hurley trying to arrange a pardon for you and Sundance?'

'Oh yeah, Johnny,' Butch smiled. 'I guess that Jacob had no luck.'

'Well, actually,' Johnny's excitement increased, 'Jacob wants to meet up with you.'

Butch looked surprised, then he asked, 'Why doesn't he just come to the ranch?'

'I told him that you wanted to keep it a secret from Sundance ... He wants to meet you in two days at the old abandoned cabin at Red Creek.'

The old abandoned cabin was about twenty miles east of the ranch near to the red fork of the Powder River.

Butch, however, was unsure about meeting Hurley. He felt guilty at not telling his partner, and he felt certain that Hurley would not be able to obtain a pardon for both himself and Sundance.

Seeing Butch's hesitation, Johnny asked anxiously, 'You will go and meet him, won't you?'

'I don't know ... '

Johnny looked crestfallen. He had a lot of respect and liking for Butch and Sundance, and he wanted them to stay on the ranch and to keep running it. He hoped that if they did manage to get a pardon from Jacob Hurley, then they would be able to do that.

'You can at least meet up with him,' Johnny pleaded, 'and hear what he has to say.'

Butch smiled, and feeling sorry for Johnny, he said, 'OK, I'll go and meet him, but don't tell Sundance; I'll tell him when I get back.'

Johnny nodded and with a happy smile, he said, 'It'll work out OK, you'll see.'

5

Butch dismounted outside of the old abandoned cabin at Red Creek, and tied his horse to the hitch rail outside. He felt very sceptical about Hurley's chances of getting them a pardon, but because of Johnny's pleadings he had agreed to the meeting.

Butch had told Sundance nothing about the meeting or the pardon. He wanted to surprise his partner with, hopefully, some good news.

Their ranch was doing well, and Butch secretly hoped for the pardon so that they would no longer be wanted by the law, at least not in Wyoming, and he also hoped that it would stop Joe Latham from ceaselessly hunting them.

Butch still felt a little guilty about not telling Sundance about the pardon, but he would do so as soon as the meeting with Jacob Hurley was over, and he had ridden back to the ranch.

The door of the abandoned cabin suddenly swung open from behind Butch and interrupted his thoughts.

Butch turned round with a cheery smile on his face; he was expecting to see Jacob Hurley standing there.

It was not, however, Jacob Hurley, but someone who caused Butch's head to whirl in shock.

It was US Marshal Joe Latham, and in Latham's right hand was a gun which he grinningly aimed at Butch.

'Don't move, Cassidy!' he shouted out.

For a few seconds, Butch was so shocked at seeing Latham to react that he stood staring numbly at the marshal, and at the gun he held.

Latham stepped up closer to the outlaw until he was only a few feet away, the grin still on his face.

'Get your hands up,' Latham rasped to the dumbfounded outlaw.

The full horror of what he had done suddenly filled Butch's mind as the shock at seeing Latham began to wear off. He had forgotten to be careful, and it was not only his own life and freedom at risk, it was Sundance's too.

'I said get your hands up, Cassidy,' Latham rasped again. 'I ain't alone here, I got deputies nearby.'

Butch did not know if Latham was lying about that, but he slowly raised his hands as he tried to think of something that he could do to distract Latham long enough for him to try and make a rush at the marshal.

'We meet again, Marshal,' Butch began mildly.

Latham refused to be put off by Butch's mild voice, and losing his grin, he growled, 'Raise your hands higher, Cassidy, above your head — now!'

Butch felt an inward groan as he raised his hands high above his head. Dealing with Latham was going to be a hard task. He would have to play along with the marshal until he had a chance to try something.

Latham reached out and took Butch's

gun from his holster, then placed it down his own gunbelt.

Butch sighed. 'So,' he said, 'it was all a set-up.'

'That's right,' Latham relaxed a little. 'And it worked, didn't it?'

'Is Johnny in on it?' Butch asked sadly. He could not believe that Johnny would set him up.

Latham hesitated, but then he grinned again and said, 'I could lie to you, but seeing as I've got you at last, and you won't escape from me again, I'll tell you the truth: Johnny ain't in on this. I met up with him about a couple of weeks ago in Casper, and pretended to be friendly with him to try to get to you and Sundance. The naïve fool that he is, he believed that I had changed, and he told me about the pardon that Hurley was trying to arrange for you and Sundance. I offered to help in some way, and again Johnny believed me.'

Butch smiled. Johnny was not guilty of betrayal, just of being too trusting.

'And I'm guessing that Jacob Hurley knows nothing about this,' Butch said, thinking of his governor friend.

'No, he don't.' Latham's grin faded, and his voice was harsh. 'He knows nothing about this trap. When Johnny told you to meet Hurley here, he was just giving you the information that he thought I was relaying to him from Hurley. Jacob Hurley is actually still trying for a pardon for you and Sundance, but that don't matter now, does it — you'll be in jail soon, or hanging from a rope.'

'Is that all that's in it for you?' Butch asked him quietly. 'To catch me and hang me?'

'I've been after you for a long time.' Latham spoke in a hard tone. 'You and that partner of yours. I was hoping that you'd both turn up here, but now that I've got you, I'll soon get Sundance.'

Butch's felt his heart almost stop beating at Latham's words. He had acted very carelessly and he was fully aware that he had placed Sundance at risk of being captured as well; he knew that Latham could use him as bait for The Kid.

Butch knew that he had to try

something soon. He could not let Latham get his partner too. Their last encounter with Marshal Latham was still vivid in his mind. The marshal had come very close to hanging them both.

Latham was watching Butch with amusement, and asked, 'Are you thinking of putting on another show for me?' He was also thinking of their last encounter and referring to the act of being terrified of hanging that Butch had put on.

Butch took a deep breath. Latham was close enough to the outlaw for Butch to rush him, and so, not letting Latham's threat of having deputies nearby deter him, and forgetting that he was still recovering from a recent bullet injury, Butch made a sudden charge at Latham.

Butch's surprise charge knocked the marshal off his feet, causing the lawman to drop his gun.

Butch had Latham at a disadvantage, and he had the upper hand, but before he could follow up on this, a sudden and crippling pain from his recent chest wound caused him to falter and to gasp.

Seeing Butch hesitate and gasp, and realizing that the outlaw was not at full strength, Latham quickly got to his feet, and after hastily grabbing his gun off the ground and putting it back in his holster, he lunged at Butch and grabbed hold of him. He was incensed at how Butch had rushed him so easily, and wanted to take the outlaw without having to use his gun.

He dragged Butch over to the cabin and flung him hard against a side wall of the wooden building and held him there with a tight grip on his upper arms.

Butch's back was up against the hard, wooden surface of the cabin, and his strength was failing, but he tried to struggle free. Latham bunched up his right fist and rammed two hard blows to Butch's stomach.

The blows caught Butch's chest wound, and the pain was horrendous. He gasped and almost collapsed, but Latham held him upright against the cabin wall, and then grabbed hold of each of Butch's wrists in a painful grip of steel.

Gasping with the pain from his chest

wound and his wrists, Butch tried to push the marshal off, but a cruelly grinning Latham kept his agonizing hold on Butch's wrists, and Butch was powerless to resist as Latham forced his wrists wide apart, outstretching Butch's arms a little. And then, in one swift movement, Latham raised Butch's wrists up higher to just above the outlaw's head and then slammed them back hard against the surface of the rough cabin wall and held them there pinned to the cabin wall just inches above Butch's head.

'Got you, Cassidy!' the marshal cried out in triumph.

Butch could not move. Latham had his wrists pinned securely to the rough surface of the cabin wall.

Latham felt confident that Butch could not struggle free.

Butch stood gasping from Latham's hard blows to his stomach; throbs of severe pain were coming from his chest wound, which had started to bleed, and he felt like he was trapped, like he was in a situation that he could not escape from.

Latham's grip on his wrists was restricting the circulation. Butch was also painfully aware of his humiliating position, which was what Latham had hoped — one of his intentions was to humiliate the outlaw.

Latham took pleasure in hurting and humiliating prisoners that had angered him in some way. Butch and Sundance had escaped when the marshal had tried to hang them, and they had also left him tied to a tree, and Latham was going to make Butch pay for that.

'You just got lucky, Latham,' Butch gasped, 'that's all.'

'Oh, yeah?' Latham grinned. 'Well, let's just see if you can get out of this. What act can you put on now?'

Butch tried to struggle, but he could not free his wrists from Latham's iron grip.

Butch brought his right knee up to try to knee the marshal in the groin, but Latham saw what he was doing and stamped down hard on Butch's right foot, causing a moan of pain from the outlaw.

Butch did not give up, and tried to kick out at Latham, but the lawman avoided his kicks and any other attempts to knee him in the groin, and he warned Butch that if he did not stop, then he would kick back harder, and in a place that Butch would not like.

Butch felt weak and in almost unbearable pain from his chest wound and the crushing hold that Latham had on his wrists, and he knew that Latham had the upper hand.

Latham stood grinning mockingly at the outlaw as Butch gave up kicking out, and tried again and again to free his wrists from Latham's powerful hold, but to no avail. Latham kept his grip and increased the pressure of his hold.

Butch groaned in agony. His wrists felt as though they were being tightened in a vice and beads of sweat streaked his forehead.

Latham's grin widened. He knew for certain that he had got the outlaw. He knew that he could have just pounded Butch with hard blows to his body and face until he was unconscious, but the sadistic marshal wanted to fully humiliate the outlaw. He wanted Butch to surrender to him, and he wanted to hear Butch say that he surrendered.

'Give up, Cassidy,' Latham sneered. 'Stop struggling and surrender. I've got you and you know it.'

Butch did not say anything in reply, he was panting from his efforts to break free, and his usually bright eyes were dim from weakness and pain. He suddenly yearned for the appearance of his partner, but Sundance did not even know where he was.

'I have got you, haven't I?' Latham sneered again.

The marshal did not get any answer from Butch, but he could see the embarrassment and dejection in Butch's eyes.

'Well, you're not denying it,' Latham smirked.

He stood looking at Butch for a few minutes. He was enjoying Butch's helplessness, and his pain and humiliation.

'You humiliated me, Cassidy,' Latham said harshly, 'you left me tied to a tree.'

'That wasn't done to humiliate you,'

Butch gasped out.

Latham snorted. 'Well, I'm doing this to humiliate you, and I think it's working.'

Latham knew that he would not have been able to humiliate the stoic Sundance Kid, but Butch was not The Kid.

Butch looked away from Latham's gloating eyes. He felt close to passing out from the pain.

Latham was torturing him.

'I see you've stopped struggling.' Latham grinned. 'Do you give up?'

Butch did not answer, adding to his pain and humiliation was the guilt he felt at knowing that whatever Latham had in store for him, he had walked unthinking into a trap, and ruined the future for himself, Sundance, and their ranch. He tried to take his mind off the pain by trying to guess at what the marshal was going to do to him. He wondered if Latham was going to hang him or use him to lure Sundance into a trap. He looked back at Latham, and, still gasping with the pain, he asked, 'Are you going to hang me?'

Latham laughed harshly, 'I reckon you'd rather that than the agony you're suffering now.'

Latham was right. The pressure he was putting on Butch's wrists was torture to the outlaw.

'Just say that you surrender, Cassidy,' Latham grinned, 'and I'll ease the pressure on your wrists.'

Latham's words barely registered with Butch; all that Butch could think about was the pain that he was going through, and the risk that he had caused to his partner.

Joe Latham suddenly felt impatient. He was determined to make Butch feel fully humiliated, and to make the outlaw say that he surrendered.

Still keeping his agonizing hold on Butch's wrists and keeping them pinned back against the cabin wall, Latham began to force Butch's wrists up higher, scraping Butch's knuckles against the wooden wall as he did so, and then he forced Butch's wrists closer together until the palms of his hands were almost touching. Latham then clasped his left hand around both wrists, holding them tightly together above the outlaw's head, and suddenly whipped out his gun from his holster with his right hand.

Latham had not wanted to use the gun, but he felt that he had no other choice. He dug the gun into Butch's sore ribs, causing a sharp cry of pain from the outlaw and shouted out, 'You can say you surrender, Cassidy, or you can die right now!'

Butch could see it in the marshal's crazed eyes that Latham was not fooling, and he knew that he could not break free from his grip. It was thinking of Sundance that caused Butch to give in. Butch would gladly give his life for The Kid, but he realized that if he did let Latham kill him at that moment, then Sundance would only go recklessly gunning for the lawman, and would most certainly get killed, and Butch did not want that to happen. He felt guilty enough for going to the meeting at Red Creek without a word to Sundance, and for walking into Latham's trap.

To surrender was Butch's only option. Maybe if he did what Latham wanted, then the marshal might just take him in without attempting to hang him or shoot him. Butch knew that Sundance would risk everything to rescue him from jail, but at least that way, Sundance would have the chance to think up some sort of rescue plan.

'OK,' Butch gasped to Latham, 'you win, I surrender.'

Latham beamed at Butch's words — he was enjoying watching Butch suffer — and he said, 'Say it again, but louder.'

Butch groaned. Latham was really taking immense delight in Butch's suffering and humiliation.

'I surrender,' Butch gasped out again as loud as he could; knowing that he was doing it for his partner helped Butch through it all.

Latham beamed again, and stayed as he was for a moment, gripping Butch's wrists and digging the gun into Butch's ribs.

The marshal looked mockingly into Butch's pain-filled eyes, then he said harshly, 'I'll let go of your wrists now, Cassidy, and I want to see you surrender. Keep your hands above your head, press your palms together, and interlock your fingers.'

Latham released his grip, and Butch sucked in his breath as some circulation returned to his wrists, but the pain grew more intense and he almost dropped his arms.

Latham cried out, 'Keep your hands above your head, press your palms together, and interlock your fingers, now!'

With an effort, Butch pressed the palms of his hands firmly together and interlocked his fingers in a prayer-like position above his head. He felt dizzy with the pain from his chest wound and the throbbing of his wrists and close to losing consciousness.

Latham gave a smug laugh, satisfied that Butch's humiliation was complete. 'Don't move, Cassidy,' he growled. 'Stay back against the cabin wall and keep your fingers interlocked.'

Butch stood back against the cabin; he was glad for something to lean against. He stayed as he was, with his palms pressed together above his head and his fingers interlocked. He saw Latham's smug eyes and his feeling of humiliation intensified and his pale face suddenly flushed red.

Latham did not hide his amusement as he saw the sudden flush of red appear in Butch's cheeks. 'Well, Cassidy,' he mocked the outlaw, 'do you feel as foolish as you look? There's no fun in surrendering, is there?'

Butch looked away, and Latham suddenly called out to his deputies who had been hiding nearby in the cover of some trees in a small copse a few yards behind the cabin, waiting for his call.

'Wade, Jeb!' Latham called. 'Come on out, I've got Cassidy!'

Jeb Taylor and Wade Ashton came out from the cover of the trees, and with their guns drawn they hurried over to Latham and Butch.

The two deputies stared in surprise at Butch standing still in surrender against the cabin wall with his palms pressed together above his head and Latham's gun digging in his ribs.

Huge red marks showed vividly on Butch's wrists, and they throbbed with excruciating pain as the circulation continued to return. There was also a widening red stain on his shirt as his chest wound continued to seep blood, and his knuckles were scratched and bleeding.

'He looks kinda foolish, don't he?' Latham smiled at his deputies.

The deputies nodded, sniggering at Butch's humiliating position.

'Did he put up a fight?' Ashton asked.

'Not much of one,' Latham answered smugly.

The marshal then instructed his deputies to keep Butch covered as he searched him. Taylor and Ashton kept their guns aimed at Butch and he stood still as the marshal took his time in searching him, adding to his humiliation. He felt the amused eyes of the deputies boring into him, and their guns ready for any movement.

Butch yearned again for the appearance of his partner, but he knew that was not going to happen; Sundance had no idea about what was happening to him.

Latham's hands were deliberately rough as he thoroughly searched Butch for any hidden weapons. He pressed hard on Butch's chest wound causing the outlaw to cry out in pain and almost fall over.

'Stand still!' Latham cried.

Somehow, Butch kept still, upright, and conscious.

The marshal took a knife from out of Butch's belt, which he passed to Jeb Taylor. He then stood back with his deputies and surveyed his prisoner with a gloating smile while aiming his gun at him.

'It don't look like you're gonna get out of this, does it, Cassidy?' he mocked.

Butch knew unhappily that he was to blame for everything that was happening to him. He had walked into this trap without a word to The Kid, and now there was no way out. They had him, but what worried him most was the fate of his partner.

Latham took a pair of handcuffs from the back of his belt and said to Butch, 'You know what happens now, don't you, Cassidy?'

A feeling of hopelessness started to spread through Butch; it looked as though Latham was not going to hang him, but keep him as bait for The Kid, and he felt tears in his eyes as he almost prayed for a miracle.

Butch had hoped that his life as a rancher alongside his partner would last for a couple of years or more. They had made a success of their ranch.

'Turn around and face the cabin!' Latham's harsh voice broke into his thoughts. 'Keep your hands high and clasped together.'

Butch hesitated, worrying about The Kid. Going to jail or being hanged did not worry him as much as the fate of his partner did.

Latham began to squeeze back the

trigger of his gun. 'First your kneecaps,' he said menacingly, 'then I'll shoot other parts of you until I finally put a bullet in your brain, so you'd better turn around and face the cabin wall.'

Still Butch hesitated. The risk that he had caused to Sundance was all that he could think about, but he gloomily realized that letting Latham kill him would not help to resolve anything, so with a heavy heart Butch slowly turned around.

'Glad you saw sense,' Latham's voice was sarcastic.

Latham kept his finger on the trigger covering Butch as he asked his deputies if anyone had followed the outlaw.

A slight smile touched Butch's pallid face; he was not the only one thinking about The Sundance Kid.

'No,' brawny Jeb Taylor answered. 'We've been watching the trail — there's no sign of anyone else.'

Latham breathed easier. He relaxed the pressure that he had on the trigger, and said with confidence to Butch, 'Now that we've got you, Cassidy, we'll soon have your partner. We'll use you to set a trap for him.'

'Sundance won't walk into any trap,' Butch told Latham, his voice weak with pain. 'He's too smart for you.'

Butch knew that The Kid would try to rescue him, but it was very unlikely that he would walk into a trap. His partner's instincts for danger were uncanny.

Latham only snorted, and handed the handcuffs to Taylor. 'You cuff him, Jeb, and I'll keep him covered.'

Jeb nodded, replaced his gun back inside his holster, and told Butch to slowly place his hands behind his back.

Rosa's long, dark auburn hair gleamed in the sun and tumbled around her shoulders. She looked so pretty, Johnny thought as he watched her doing some washing in a tub outside the ranch house.

It was a lovely sunny morning as Johnny strode over to Rosa. He had not attempted to tell her again of his feelings for her since he had been abruptly interrupted at the back of the blacksmith shop by Rocky

Moran. He had been awaiting his chance and trying to summon up the nerve.

Rosa turned around and smiled at Johnny, and the lad felt flustered, and instead of telling her what was in his heart, he told her instead about Butch's meeting that morning with Jacob Hurley.

About an hour had passed since Butch had ridden out to Red Creek, and because Butch could not and would not lie to his partner, he had told Johnny to inform The Kid that he was riding off to visit a nearby ranch.

Rosa carried on smiling at Johnny as he told her about the meeting and the pardon; she too hoped that Hurley would be able to arrange a pardon for the outlaws. Sundance meant a lot to her, but what Johnny said next caused her face to change and her eyes to widen in alarm.

Johnny had said that his father, US Marshal Joe Latham, had helped him to set up the meeting.

'Oh, Johnny, no!' Rosa cried.

'It's OK, Rosa,' Johnny smiled, 'Pa's changed — '

'How can you believe that?' Rosa cried out again. 'He tried to hang Butch and Sundance not long back!'

'He's different now,' Johnny still smiled. He did not understand Rosa's concern.

Rosa did not wait to hear any more. She raced off to find Sundance.

The young horse in the corral stood watching Sundance with suspicion as, talking gently to it, Sundance strapped on the saddle. After weeks of training, this was the first time that the horse had felt a saddle on his back. He had been trained to accept the bridle and the feel of a bit in his mouth.

Sundance then stepped back and let the horse pace around the corral, getting used to the feel of the saddle.

Ranch-hand Mark Casey stood outside the corral watching intently. His attention suddenly turned to Rosa as she ran up to the corral.

Ignoring Mark, Rosa screamed Sundance's name from outside of the fence.

'Go away!' Sundance snapped at her without turning to look at her, his eyes still on the young horse.

Rosa cried out, 'Butch is in trouble!'

The Kid turned to look at her. She had gained some of his attention, but he did not attempt to leave the corral or the horse, he just asked, 'How is he in trouble, he's gone to the Hemming ranch, hasn't he?'

'No!' Rosa shook her head wildly. 'He's gone to Red Creek!'

Sundance's eyes flashed, he walked across to the corral fence and jumped over it.

'Why has he gone to Red Creek?' he demanded harshly of Rosa just as Johnny ran up to them.

Rosa quickly told him about Jacob Hurley and the pardon, and then about Joe Latham's involvement.

Johnny almost fainted on the spot at the look in The Kid's eyes.

Sundance grabbed hold of Johnny by both arms, and shook the lad as he said in intense fury, 'If your father hangs Butch, then you'd better run and hide, because I'll do the same thing to you!'

Johnny tried to speak, but he could not get any words out, he was too scared.

Sundance then thrust the terrified boy aside, and after telling Mark to carry on training the young horse, he raced to the stables.

He was full of mixed emotions as he led his horse out of the stables and swung up into the saddle. He was furious at Butch for not having told him about the pardon and the meeting with Jacob Hurley, but the fury he felt was nothing compared to his fear for his partner's life.

As Sundance galloped quickly away from the ranch, he heard the sound of thundering hoofs behind him, and he knew without looking that Rosa and Johnny were following him.

For the first part of the trail to Red Creek, Rosa and Johnny kept pace with Sundance, but then they came to a fork in the trail. If they followed the main trail it would take them a lot longer to reach

Red Creek, but it was an easier, more well-defined trail to ride. If they took the other trail, the one known as Dead Man's Trail, then it would take over ten miles off the distance, but it was also known as the suicide trail. Even very experienced riders were reluctant to use it.

The Kid did not hesitate; he turned his horse on to Dead Man's Trail. Rosa and Johnny held back at first, but then followed him.

The trail was hazardous. It was an extremely narrow, rock-strewn pathway. It was more like a ledge with huge rocks and hills on one side, and a drop of hundreds of feet on the other. It was known to have frequent landslides and rockslides.

The trail got even narrower, and Rosa and Johnny became anxious and would not go on any further. They turned their horses around and rode back to where the trail had forked.

The Kid kneed his horse onwards. He and Butch had ridden the trail together and knew part of it quite well; they had not followed it all the way to the end, though, so Sundance did not know what dangers to expect, but he knew he had to carry on. If he had any chance of getting to Butch before Latham could hang him, then he had to continue to the end of Dead Man's Trail.

The narrow ledge that Sundance rode upon became narrower and narrower and seemed about to disappear altogether, but then, he saw that several yards ahead of him, the trail widened.

Riding along the last few inches of the narrow trail was torture for The Kid and his horse. The horse slipped a few times on the rocky pathway, but Sundance refused to stop and turn back. All that mattered to him was getting to Butch. He kept his nerve and encouraged his horse along.

The Kid was halfway to the safety of the wider trail ahead when he heard a rumbling sound: it was the start of a landslide. In a matter of seconds, the rocks and ground higher up in the hills started to give way, and great stones came crashing down. They missed Sundance by inches.

The Kid knew that he had to move out of the way fast before yet more boulders could crash down and he dug his spurs in and gave out a wild yell to signal his horse to charge forwards.

The horse, although feeling jittery, responded to his yell and charged swiftly forward to where the trail widened. Behind Sundance came a tremendous roar as an avalanche of stones and boulders fell to the ground.

Butch had started to obey Jeb Taylor's order to place his hands behind his back when a low whistle coming from a group of huge broken rocks to the right of the cabin suddenly stopped him, and he just held his hands raised above his head.

It was a whistle that Butch would know anywhere, a whistle that was a signal to him alone. For a fraction of a second he could not really believe it, and then he felt everything inside of him suddenly shout for joy. He no longer felt like passing out, and the unceasing pain from his chest wound and throbbing wrists seemed to lessen. The relief and joy Butch felt was immeasurable.

His miracle had happened.

It was a whistle from The Sundance Kid, the partner who had never let him down.

Somehow Sundance must have found out about the trap and was there somewhere near the cabin. Butch realized that to get there as quickly as he had done, his intrepid partner must have ridden along the Dead Man's Trail.

The low whistle caused some concern to Latham, and he looked to the right of him where the whistle had seemed to come from. He saw nothing but the broken rocks.

Latham said angrily to his deputies, 'I thought you said that no one followed him!'

'We saw no one!' Ashton cried.

The deputies had not seen Sundance because they had stopped watching out for anyone following Butch at the time that The Kid had ridden up to the cabin, and no one had heard The Kid's horse approaching due to Sundance dismounting and leading the animal into the cover of the rocks.

The thought that the Sundance Kid might be close by and about to make a move to rescue his partner had unnerved all three lawmen, even Latham.

Latham cursed, and feeling very uneasy, said to Jeb Taylor, 'Get the cuffs on him quick, and get him into the cabin!'

A nervous Jeb again ordered Butch to place his hands behind his back.

Butch slowly started to lower his hands. He placed them behind his back. His previous feeling of hopelessness had disappeared, and he felt a lot more cheerful and optimistic as he waited for his partner to make his move.

Opening out the handcuffs, Taylor grabbed hold of Butch's wrists.

Butch stifled a cry of pain at Taylor's hold on his painful wrists. He did not want Sundance to know yet how badly he had been hurt. He knew what Sundance's reaction was likely to be, and he wanted to avoid more trouble.

Before Taylor could apply the handcuffs, however, there was a loud cracking sound as a shot rang out.

The bullet landed close to the feet of Latham and his deputies. Dust flew up around the feet of the three men, and they turned to look at the imposing figure of the Sundance Kid.

Taylor held tight to Butch's wrists.

Latham and Ashton still kept hold of their guns, but made no attempt to fire them.

Sundance had come out from the cover of the rocks about fifteen feet to the right of them, and he had moved into a position from where he could handle everything that went on. In his right hand, he held his Colt Peacemaker gun.

'You two drop your guns!' were the harsh, commanding words of The Kid to Latham and Ashton.

'And you, Taylor!' he called fiercely to Jeb Taylor. 'Let go of my partner and move away from him. You ain't taking him anywhere.'

A happy smile briefly touched Butch's pale face; he was so glad to hear his partner's commanding voice.

No one moved.

Another crack of gunfire came from The Kid's Colt, and more dust flew about. The bullet landed even closer to the feet of the three lawmen.

Fear began to show on the faces of Ashton and Taylor.

Trying to hide his own slight involuntary nervousness, Latham told his men to stay where they were. As tough and as powerfully built as he was, even Latham felt a little apprehensive of The Kid.

The marshal glowered at Sundance and said, 'If you fire again, you might hit your partner.'

'If I fire again, I will kill, and it won't be my partner,' was Sundance's icy promise.

His merciless grey-blue eyes and chilling words sent fear through Taylor and Ashton.

Jeb Taylor immediately let go of Butch's wrists and moved a few feet away. Ashton dropped his gun and followed Taylor.

Both deputies raised their hands high.

Latham did not move. He still stood close to Butch, and he still held his gun.

Butch turned around to smile at The Kid, and to say with feeling, 'Am I glad to see you.'

Butch did not care that Latham still stood close to him, or that the marshal still held his gun. He knew that Sundance had them all under his firm control.

Sundance was still angry with Butch, but he became concerned by his partner's appearance. Butch's smile had been weak and his face was almost ashen, and there was a wide bloodstain on Butch's shirt from his earlier bullet injury, which appeared to be still bleeding. Butch looked close to collapsing.

'Are you OK?' Sundance asked his partner.

Butch noticed the angry glint as well as the concern in Sundance's eyes, and he knew that he was in for a tongue-lashing from The Kid later. 'I'll live, I guess,' Butch said as lightly as he could.

Sundance frowned. Butch's lightly

spoken answer did not fool him; his partner was obviously in pain. He stared hard at Latham. He felt like giving the man a vicious beating.

The marshal stood seething, but not moving — he knew better than to try anything against Sundance.

'Drop your gun, Latham!' Sundance snapped. 'Move away from my partner, and raise your hands.'

Latham made no effort to move, and a sneer appeared on his face.

Sundance stepped closer to the lawman, his gun never wavering as he said quietly, but menacingly, 'What was it you were saying to Butch, Latham? Something about first the kneecaps, and then other body parts … ?'

The Kid had led his horse into the cover of the rocks at Red Creek at about the same time as Latham was making that very same threat to Butch.

The sneer faded from Latham's face. The Kid's threat was real; he heard it in the outlaw's voice. Uttering a bitter curse, he dropped his weapon. He stepped away from Butch, and raised his hands high.

Butch moved away from the cabin wall, and started to search the three men. His movements were slow and painful. He could feel the ache from his chest wound and wrists starting to intensify again. He then retrieved his own weapons from Latham.

The marshal gave Butch a mocking grin.

Butch ignored the grin, and said with a hint of pride in his voice, 'I told you that my partner was smarter than you, didn't I, Latham?'

Latham grunted.

Butch went inside the cabin and found some rope, which he used to tie the deputies' hands behind their backs. He used the handcuffs to secure Latham's wrists behind him, flinching as he did it. His wrists were obviously hurting him. They still had vivid red marks on them and were starting to swell.

Sundance noticed Butch's wrists and asked sharply, 'What did he do to you, partner?'

'It's nothing,' Butch murmured, avoiding The Kid's eyes.

There was something in Butch's voice that perturbed The Kid. He could tell that his partner seemed very unhappy about something. The Kid was right in his thinking. Butch still felt deep humiliation at the way that Latham had treated him.

'What did he do to you?' Sundance asked again, and in an even sharper tone.

'Let it go,' Butch replied, still avoiding The Kid's eyes.

Sundance had no intention of letting it go. Something had happened between Butch and Latham. Something that he could tell had upset Butch considerably, and he was determined that Latham would not get away with it.

'I think it's time that someone inflicted pain on you, Latham,' Sundance said quietly but with intent to the marshal.

'Would that someone be you?' Latham grinned.

'Yeah,' Sundance said icily, 'it surely would.' He told Butch to unlock the handcuffs that secured Latham's wrists.

Sundance's intention was clear, he was going to slug it out with the Marshal.

'No, Kid — ' Butch almost begged, and he refused to unlock the handcuffs. Although he had complete faith in his partner, he was not too happy at the thought of watching him fight Latham.

'Then give me the key!' Sundance snapped. 'I'll do it!'

'No, Kid,' Butch appealed to his partner, 'it was mostly my pride he — ' He did not finish his words as a sudden intense stab of pain from his chest wound caused him to catch his breath and clutch at his chest, blood trickling through his fingers. He began to sway on his feet, and he stepped away from Latham in case he passed out.

Sundance watched him anxiously. Butch was clearly not in a good state health-wise. The thin stream of blood seeping through his partner's fingers worried The Kid, and he decided against putting Butch through the ordeal of watching him fight it out with Latham.

Butch was still swaying on his feet

while holding his chest wound and gasping. Sundance went over to him and held him steady for a few seconds. 'Find somewhere to sit,' he said sharply, 'before you fall down.'

There was a raised wooden platform attached to the front of the cabin, and Butch limped over to it and sat down. He breathed slowly and painfully and clutched his throbbing chest wound.

Sundance put his Colt away. He was standing close to Latham, and the marshal said with a snigger, 'So, you've changed your mind about slugging it out with me.'

Sundance turned cold, angry eyes on Latham and he struck the lawman hard across the face with his hand.

Butch called out in a weak and painful voice from where he sat on the wooden platform, 'I told you before, Latham, not to push my partner.'

Latham was knocked off balance and he fell to the ground. He landed awkwardly in the dirt on his side and rolled over on to his back. Sundance had not used his fist on the marshal, but there was still a small cut under Latham's right eye.

Sundance said scathingly to him, 'You kicked my partner when he lay tied up on the ground.'

A sudden spark of fear flared in Latham's eyes.

Sundance, his voice quiet, but deadly serious, said, 'I'm not such a coward as to kick a helpless man, Latham, but one more sound out of you and I might change my mind.'

Latham looked about to comment, but the fierce, unforgiving look in Sundance's eyes stopped him, and he lay still and silent.

Sundance walked over to where Butch sat on the platform. His partner was still very pale-faced, and pain glistened in his eyes, but he was not holding his chest wound any more, and he gave The Kid a faint smile before asking, 'What shall we do with them?'

Sundance sighed deeply. The only way they would be free of the threat of Joe Latham was to kill him, but they could not do that, so he said to Butch, 'We'll stick them on their horses and head them towards Casper.'

Butch thought it over and then nodded. Casper was the closest town and about three days' ride away, but about halfway to Casper was the blacksmith shop and general store of Jasper and Jesse Sheldon.

Sundance fetched the horses of the three lawman from where they had been tethered in some thick bushes near to the cabin, and he helped them to mount the animals. He tied the feet of each man together underneath their horse's stomachs before leading the horses on to the trail that led to Casper.

Latham gave The Kid a loathsome look, but he did not say anything.

Sundance gave each horse a thump to start them trotting along the trail.

The Kid went back to where Butch sat outside the cabin. He sat down beside his partner and said, 'I don't think that's the last we have seen of Latham and his deputies.'

'I know,' Butch said in a glum voice

that was very unlike him.

The fact that Joe Latham was so determined to capture the two outlaws was one of the main reasons Butch had hoped that Hurley could arrange a pardon for them: he wanted to get Latham off their backs.

Sundance knew that his partner was hurt and in pain, but he had to voice his anger.

'What the hell do you think you were doing?' he suddenly asked angrily, staring hard at Butch. 'What did I say to you about being careful?'

Butch lowered his head. He could feel The Kid's anger.

'You are damned lucky that Johnny let slip to Rosa about what you were doing, and that she had the good sense to tell me!' Sundance rasped.

'I'm sorry, partner,' Butch said quietly without lifting his head.

'You do know that Latham could have strung you up before I got here, don't you?' Sundance fumed.

Butch nodded. He still stared

downwards. He understood why Sundance felt so angry. He had behaved very irresponsibly.

'Did your brain suddenly stop working?' Sundance fumed again.

Butch said nothing.

'Did it?' Sundance yelled.

'I guess it did,' Butch said in a dismal tone. He lifted his head. He looked into Sundance's angry eyes and tried to explain his actions by saying, 'I wasn't expecting Latham to be here. I was expecting Jacob Hurley and I hoped to give you some good news ... '

Sundance did not say anything, he looked away from Butch. He was still fuming, but he tried to hold his tongue. He was thinking of Butch's vulnerable side. He knew that his partner could be emotionally distressed for weeks by angry and cruel words from people that he cared about.

'I didn't lie to you,' Butch said with sincerity. 'You know I would never lie to you. I just didn't tell you about the pardon because I didn't want to get your hopes up. I was hoping that we could get this pardon and not be wanted men in Wyoming any more. That way we could really make a go of the ranch, and maybe keep Latham off our backs.' He stopped speaking for a moment, and then said with genuine remorse, 'I'm truly sorry, Sundie, I don't know what else to say, except I acted very stupidly and I know that I put us both at risk.'

Sundance still looked away from Butch, and he did not speak.

Butch started to say something, but he had to stop. He gave a low moan as pain from his chest wound stabbed at him again.

Sundance turned to look at Butch again, and his anger abated as he looked at his partner's pallid complexion and pain-filled eyes, at his swollen wrists and blood-stained shirt.

'I reckon I can understand why you did it,' The Kid finally said. 'You weren't to know that Johnny would tell his father.'

Butch said in low voice, 'If it helps

you to feel any less angry, knowing that I put you at risk hurt me far more than anything Latham did.'

The Kid smiled slightly, and said with a warning in his voice, 'Just don't go riding off to any more meetings without telling me first, whatever they are about — OK?'

'That's a certainty,' Butch smiled, then he added quietly, 'I'm really sorry — '

'Forget it,' The Kid said abruptly, 'you've apologized enough. The main thing is I got here in time.'

Sundance opened up Butch's shirt to examine the bullet injury. It was still bleeding, but only very slightly.

Butch moaned with pain as Sundance (as he had done only a few weeks before) used his bandanna and strips of material that he ripped off Butch's shirt to bandage the wound.

'This is getting to be a habit,' Sundance said with slight annoyance.

Butch grinned weakly. 'I'll be running out of shirts soon.'

'You mean as well as your smart thinking,' Sundance stated.

Butch looked at him, and for a second he wondered if The Kid had meant it, but then he read his partner's mind and he saw the grin that Sundance was trying to hide.

'Sorry, *amigo*,' Sundance said as he stood up, 'I couldn't resist it.'

Sundance walked back into the rocks to the right of the cabin to fetch his horse.

Butch went over to the bubbling creek which was near to the cabin on the left, and kneeling down he dipped his painful wrists into the cool water. The redness had faded and the marks were now a deep purple, but the swelling was worse. The cool water brought him some relief.

Sundance returned with his horse, and tethered the animal to the hitch rail at the front of the cabin next to Butch's horse, then he stood watching Butch with anxious eyes.

'What happened with Latham?' he asked quietly. 'How did he hurt your wrists?' The Kid was wondering with concern if Latham had used some kind of weird torture.

Butch took his wrists out of the water. To him it had been torture. He still felt the sting of Latham's humiliating treatment of him, and he felt mortified at how effortlessly Latham had overpowered him and restrained him. He caught his breath as he felt another twinge of pain from his chest wound, and he got off his knees and sat down on a smooth-topped boulder near the creek.

The Kid still watched him with concerned eyes. He knew that there was something else other than the pain bothering Butch.

'Butch ... ?' The Kid asked quietly.

There was shame in Butch's voice and he could not look at The Kid as he told his partner about how Latham had humiliated him with the agonizing hold on his wrists and by forcing him to say that he surrendered.

There was only one person in the world that Butch would ever give a detailed account to of everything that had happened between himself and Latham, and that person was The Kid.

Several times as Butch was speaking, The Kid took deep breaths of anger; he could tell by his partner's voice how humiliated and dejected Butch had felt at the time.

Sundance was angry at the way that Latham had humiliated Butch, and if Butch had told him earlier, then Sundance would have given Latham the thrashing of his life. He was also angry that Butch had let Latham's sadistic behaviour make him feel so ashamed.

If it had been Sundance whom Latham had tried to humiliate, then he would not have succeeded. The Kid had too tough an exterior and interior to ever feel anything like humiliation or much else, but Butch was different.

Butch was fearless in any kind of danger and could face up to anything and anyone, and Sundance respected and admired his partner immensely, but Butch had a vulnerable and sensitive side, and he could feel certain things like humiliation very intensely.

'You're the only person I'll ever tell

this to.' Butch spoke forlornly, and he still could not look at his partner as he added, 'So now, you can yell at me again for letting Latham get to me.'

Butch knew that his unemotional and extremely tough partner would not have been affected at all by any kind of humiliation, and he knew that Sundance was probably angry with him for letting Latham upset him so much.

The Kid sighed. 'Yeah, I could yell at you again,' he said with a trace of anger in his voice, 'and I feel like doing it, but I won't.'

It really bothered him to see Butch looking so down, and to see that his partner felt too ashamed to look at him.

The Kid walked over to where Butch sat looking very dejected on the boulder, and he tried to think of something to say to help lift Butch's despondency. Sympathy and understanding did not come easily to him.

He squeezed his partner's shoulder and said quietly, but with a firm edge to his voice, 'Don't take what Latham did to you to heart, *amigo*, and don't feel so ashamed. You were still recovering from a bullet injury and Latham took advantage of that.' He paused, and then carried on: 'You only surrendered to him to protect me. Latham is scum compared to you. He ain't worthy enough to even wipe your boots, and it could have been much worse; he could have shot you or strung you up, and I am very thankful that he did not. Now, will you look at me … ?'

Butch smiled faintly to himself knowing how hard it must have been for Sundance to say all of that. Butch was supposed to be the smart one in their partnership, and yet, sometimes, Sundance proved to be the wisest person that he had ever known. He finally lifted his eyes to look very sheepishly at The Kid.

'You idiot,' Sundance said roughly, 'you have nothing to feel ashamed of. You are just as tough as Latham and a helluva lot braver, don't you see that?'

'Oh yes, sir,' Butch smiled at his partner, and the usual cheery sparkle was almost back in his eyes.

Suddenly, the attention of both outlaws was turned to something else. They heard the sound of horses' hoof beats thundering towards the cabin, and they looked in the direction of the main trail and spotted two riders galloping fast towards them, through the rocks, dust and trees.

'It's probably Johnny and Rosa,' Sundance remarked to Butch. 'They followed me up to Dead Man's Trail.'

The two riders galloped closer, and they were indeed Johnny and Rosa. The youngsters brought their horses to a stop close to the outlaws.

One look at Butch, who was still seated on the boulder, at the paleness of his face, his swollen wrists, and the dressing that Sundance had applied to his chest, and Johnny realized that Sundance's and Rosa's fears had been correct, and that his father had set a trap.

Johnny attempted to say that he was sorry, but when he looked into Sundance's accusing eyes, he could not get the words out.

Rosa also looked at Sundance; she was

happy to see that he had managed to ride through Dead Man's Trail all right, and she admired his stubborn courage, but knew better than to say so. The Kid did not appreciate praise, but he did sometimes grudgingly accept it from Butch.

Johnny dismounted and asked Butch if he was all right.

'What do you think?' Sundance snapped at the boy.

Johnny's eyes clouded over. He knew that The Kid had an unforgiving nature — and the outlaw had already threatened to hang him — and he said with sadness, 'I'll leave the ranch if you want me to.'

Butch did not want Johnny to leave the ranch, but he left the decision up to Sundance. He felt that he had already caused his partner enough reasons to be angry with him and he would not disagree with Sundance's decision.

The Kid stared angrily at Johnny, he realized though that the youngster had been taken in by his father, and he said curtly, 'You can stay, but only if you keep away from your father.'

Johnny brightened up. 'I will,' he gushed. 'I promise I will. I won't betray you again.'

'You better hadn't,' Sundance told him harshly, 'because if you do betray us again, intentionally or not, then I'll do what I threatened you with before.'

Johnny's brightness disappeared and Rosa looked shocked.

Butch looked down at the ground; he did not know what The Kid had threatened to do to Johnny, but he could guess.

Sundance went over to the hitch rail to untie the horses belonging to himself and Butch.

Johnny said in a whisper to Butch, 'He meant that, didn't he?'

'Yeah, he did.' Butch looked up at Johnny and Rosa. 'Sundance always means what he says. You're lucky he's giving you another chance, Johnny.'

6

The sun blazed in the Wyoming sky. It was another hot day as Johnny Latham spotted the three men walking furtively towards the ranch house and other buildings, and despite Butch giving his ranch-hands instructions to keep a lookout for uninvited guests, the unwelcome visitors had not been seen.

Johnny had been fetching water from the creek which ran along the right side of the ranch. The men had not seen him, but Johnny had seen them.

The boy stiffened with shock and horror as he recognized the men as Deputies Jeb Taylor and Wade Ashton, and his father, US Marshal Joe Latham. Johnny ducked behind a tree and watched the three men split up.

Joe Latham headed into the ranch house, brandishing a gun in his right hand.

Johnny knew that only Louisa and Hank Westwood were inside the ranch house, and they were no match for his father.

Jeb Taylor, his gun drawn, cautiously went into the barn not too many yards in front and to the right of the ranch house, and Wade Ashton, also with his gun drawn, sneakily entered the barn on the left.

Johnny guessed that Deputies Taylor and Ashton were taking up positions in the barns to keep a watch out, and to shoot anyone approaching the ranch house.

Johnny's heart started to pound and he thought quickly. He knew that Butch and Sundance were about two miles out from the ranch house with Rosa and the other ranch-hands — they were branding some of the young cattle in the corrals.

Johnny could not risk taking one of the horses out of the stables because he would be seen by Taylor and Ashton. He would have to cover the two miles distance on foot.

Keeping undercover of the thick undergrowth and bushes and trees on the right of the ranch, Johnny made his way as fast as he could to the corrals where Butch and Sundance were.

Ranch-hands Tim and Tom Turner, along with Mark Casey were busy branding some of the young cattle in one of the corrals, and the animals were bawling nosily, showing their disapproval of the branding iron.

Butch and Sundance were helping to rope and brand the cattle.

Rosa was watching from the corral fence when she saw Johnny suddenly come dashing out from the undergrowth. Breathless and hot, he collapsed at her feet.

Rosa bent over him and called out to Butch and Sundance.

Some several minutes later, after a few drinks of water from Butch's canteen, Johnny was able to tell them about Latham and his deputies being at the ranch.

An angry spark flashed in Sundance's eyes: he had been waiting to get his hands on Latham.

Butch saw the spark and he frowned. He knew what was on The Kid's mind.

At the rear of the ranch house, and keeping behind the shelter of a tangled mass of trees, rocks and sagebrush, Butch, Sundance, Johnny, and Rosa were trying to decide the best way to confront Latham and his deputies.

They agreed that they would split up to try to capture the three men.

'Leave Latham to me,' Sundance said in a no-arguments tone. He was determined to give the marshal what he so badly deserved.

'Kid — ' Butch began, looking at his partner, who was crouched down behind a rock to the left of him, and then he said no more. He knew better than to try and talk The Kid out of it.

Johnny said that he would take on Wade Ashton who had entered the barn on the left of the ranch house, and Rosa, who was sheltering behind a tree next to Johnny said that she would go with him.

Johnny looked at her anxiously. 'No,

Rosa!' he cried. 'It'll be too dangerous, you should stay here.'

'My sister is in danger,' Rosa snapped angrily, 'and you are all my friends, I will not just stand by!'

She was a very bold young lady, which was why Johnny cared for her so much.

'And anyway,' Sundance said looking towards Johnny and Rosa, 'I hope I haven't wasted all that time in teaching her to shoot; you might need her help, Johnny.'

Rosa's eyes sparkled at his words. He had faith in her.

Butch smiled — only he had noticed the sparkle in her brown eyes.

Sundance never really bothered to look closely at her. To him she was still that annoying little kid who used to follow him around at Hole-in-the-Wall.

Johnny very unwillingly agreed that Rosa could go with him to confront Ashton, and Butch stated that he would go after Jeb Taylor, who had gone into the barn on the right.

It was then decided that Butch, Johnny, and Rosa would try to capture Ashton and Taylor in the barns before Sundance went for the ranch house and Latham. They wanted to capture the deputies before they could spot Sundance going up to the ranch house.

There was a side door to the ranch house, but Sundance stated that he was going straight through the front door, and no one could persuade him otherwise.

Johnny and Rosa wished Butch and Sundance good luck, and then moved away through the mass of brush, trees, and rocks to make their approach to the barn on the left of the ranch house.

Butch looked at Sundance with worried eyes. He was thinking of suggesting that they both went after Jeb Taylor together and then Joe Latham.

Sundance read his thoughts and said to him, not too politely, 'Stop worrying. I can handle Latham. Now, get going.'

Butch hesitated and then said, 'Just be careful, partner,' and he started to move away through the brush.

Sundance called him back and said,

'Make sure you follow your own advice and you be careful too.'

Butch smiled. 'I will.'

Both of the barns were situated a few yards to the front of the ranch house, and the doors at the front of the barns were in a position that allowed a good view of the ranch house. At the rear of both barns was a trap door, and Butch wriggled through the trap door of the barn to the right of the ranch house. Holding his Colt in his hand, he slowly stood up and looked around.

The barns were used for food storage for the livestock, and sometimes for housing horses. There were a couple of empty stalls on either side of the barn and some ropes, saddles, and spurs hanging from the timber walls.

It was in the upper hayloft of the barn that Butch spotted Jeb Taylor.

The deputy was lying on his stomach in the hay looking through the small open door of the hayloft with his gun aimed and ready for action.

Taylor was oblivious to Butch's presence as he intently kept a watch over the ranch grounds.

Butch slowly and quietly climbed up the small ladder into the hayloft and stood close behind Jeb Taylor.

The deputy suddenly tensed. He lifted his gun up slightly and began to squeeze back the trigger.

Butch also went tense as he saw through the small hayloft door what Taylor had caught sight of.

It was Sundance walking boldly up to the ranch house door.

'Hold it, Taylor!' Butch rasped, causing the deputy to jump involuntary. 'Pull that trigger and I'll kill you.'

Taylor stopped squeezing the trigger, and both he and Butch watched as Sundance kicked in the ranch house door, and disappeared from their sight.

'Drop the gun!' Butch snapped at Taylor.

Taylor did not drop his gun, instead he suddenly spun over in the hay on to his back, and he let off two shots at Butch.

The bullets narrowly missed Butch as he dropped low and returned fire.

Butch shot Taylor's gun from his hand and the weapon went spinning into the hay. Aiming at Taylor, Butch told the man to turn over and lie on his stomach again, and to place his hands behind his back.

Taylor did not move.

Butch had not forgotten how Taylor had sniggered at him when Latham had forced him to surrender, and he said to the deputy in an unusually hard tone of voice, 'I can kill you or tie you up. Which is it to be?'

Unarmed, Taylor knew he had to obey. He turned over on to his stomach and placed his hands behind his back.

Butch grabbed a coil of rope from the barn wall and used it to tie Taylor's hands behind him. When he had finished, Butch said to the deputy, 'You look kinda foolish, Taylor.'

Johnny and Rosa crept through the trap door of the barn on the left of the ranch house. The interior was much the same as the other barn, with empty stalls and saddles and other equipment on the walls.

Wade Ashton was not in the hayloft, but was standing near the door of the barn at the front. He held a gun in his right hand. The huge barn door was open wide, and Ashton was peering out while trying to remain unseen.

Johnny, who also had his gun in his hand, started to creep up slowly behind Ashton. Rosa crept furtively behind Johnny.

When Johnny and Rosa were about ten feet away from Ashton, they saw the man raise his gun and start to squeeze the trigger. He had also seen Sundance.

Loud gunfire was heard a split second later, coming from the direction of the other barn.

Johnny yelled to Ashton to drop his gun and raise his hands.

Ashton swung round on them with his gun blazing.

One shot struck Johnny's arm and the lad dropped his gun.

Rosa did not hesitate; she very quickly grabbed the gun off the ground and returned fire on Ashton.

Her shooting was fast and accurate.

Ashton's gun was blasted out of his hand, bullets buzzed around him, and he yelled, 'Don't shoot any more!' He raised his hands high.

Johnny's wound was only slight and hardly bleeding, and he found some rope to tie Ashton's hands with.

The two youngsters proudly marched their prisoner out of the barn.

'You're one brave lady, Rosa,' Johnny smiled at her, 'and a good shot too.'

Rosa said with affection in her eyes, 'I had a good teacher.'

There was no gun in Sundance's hand as he swiftly kicked open the front door of the ranch house. He had no idea what awaited him inside, but he felt confident that he could handle it. All he wanted was to get his hands on Joe Latham.

Louisa and Hank were seated at the table in the centre of the living room.

They were tied to the chairs and gagged. Latham stood behind them, his back to the open brick fire place, and he held a gun on them.

The marshal had not been worried about someone entering the ranch house without him knowing; he had been relying on his two deputies in the barns to be on the lookout and to fire warning shots. He had given his deputies instructions to kill anyone they saw approaching the ranch house except Butch and Sundance. They could shoot to wound the outlaws, but not kill them. Latham intended to use his two hostages, Hank and Louisa, to force Butch and Sundance to surrender, and then he would hang them. He did not know that his two men could no longer warn him of anything.

Latham had no time to react as The Kid kicked in the door and crashed through it.

All the marshal saw was a flash of movement as Sundance darted towards him, and he desperately tried to get a shot off from his gun.

A strong kick from Sundance's right leg sent Latham's gun flying from his hand. The Kid grabbed hold of Latham by one arm and dragged him outside. He flung the lawman into the dirt, and said, 'When I've finished with you, Latham, you'll be begging to surrender!'

Gunfire was heard coming from the direction of both barns.

The Kid took his mind off Latham for a second — he was thinking of Butch.

Latham got to his feet, there was a sneer on his face as he looked at The Kid. His powerful frame had intimidated a lot of men, but he now faced an opponent who could not be intimidated.

The marshal tried to goad The Kid, by asking, 'How's your partner's wrists? He did tell you about what I did to him, didn't he?'

'You are scum compared to my partner, Latham,' Sundance said fiercely. 'Let's see how you like being humiliated!'

Latham felt some unease at The Kid's fierce words, but he told himself that he could beat this man. The two men circled each other warily, and then Latham rushed in to swing a vicious blow at The Kid's head, but Sundance saw it coming and ducked. The blow struck his shoulder instead of his head, and the impact caused him to stagger and almost fall.

Again, Latham charged in, but this time Sundance met him halfway and savagely hit out, returning blow for blow. Sundance did not try to avoid Latham's blows; he was intent only on hurting the marshal, and making the man pay for humiliating Butch.

After five minutes of slugging it out, the men broke apart. They had both taken a heavy pounding.

There was a cut on The Kid's cheek and above his right eye.

Latham's lips were split and bleeding and blood was streaming from his nose.

Their knuckles were bleeding.

Both men were warily watching each other and panting heavily.

Latham suddenly hurled himself at The Kid with a roar of rage and with fists flying.

A lesser man might have felt some fear at seeing the furious onslaught hurtling at him, but not the tough and fearless Sundance Kid. As Latham came at him, The Kid stepped up to meet him, and, flinging his left arm outwards, he knocked one of the advancing fists aside, deflecting the blow and exposing Latham's jaw. Quick as a flash, Sundance's right fist shot out with all of his massive strength behind it, and landed with a terrific, bone-crushing thud on the exposed jaw of the lawman.

Latham crashed to the ground and lay still.

Sundance stood over him wondering if he was going to get up again. He was not finished with the man yet.

As Sundance stood over Joe Latham wondering if the marshal was going to get up, Butch emerged from the barn holding the arm of his prisoner. He had put his gun away. A half-smile touched The Kid's face when he saw his partner, and Butch smiled with relief at The Kid.

Butch stayed where he was outside of

the barn, about twenty feet or so away from The Kid and Latham and he kept hold of Jeb Taylor's arm.

Johnny and Rosa came out of the barn on the left holding Wade Ashton between them as they walked over to join Butch and Taylor. Johnny had taken his gun back from Rosa and returned it to his holster. There was a small bullet graze on his arm.

Rosa headed towards the ranch house to check on her sister, passing Sundance and Latham on the way. She paused briefly to glance anxiously at Sundance, who still stood over Latham, but he told her to hurry up and get past him.

Rosa went into the ranch house and quickly untied Louisa and Hank and removed their gags. The three of them then went outside and sat down on the bench on the porch of the ranch house.

Joe Latham coughed and spluttered on the ground, then he attempted to rise, struggling to his feet. Sundance bunched up his right fist, and as Latham stood up, he struck the marshal hard in the face.

Latham fell on to his back with a grunt. The blood was flowing from numerous cuts on his face, and blood still streamed from his nose.

He made no other attempt to get up.

Sundance knelt astride the lawman and grabbed hold of his wrists with such force that Latham cried out. The Kid grinned icily as he pinned Latham's wrists to the ground, one each side of the lawman's head, and asked unfeelingly, 'Do you surrender, Latham?'

Butch realized that The Kid was humiliating and punishing Latham for him, and he called out, 'It's over, Kid, let him go.'

'It's not over yet,' Sundance called back. 'He hasn't said he surrenders yet.'

The Kid's hold on Latham's wrists was so constricting and so painful that Latham moaned a few times, but he said with a sneer, 'I'll never surrender to you.'

'That's what you think,' Sundance said coldly.

Sundance placed the palms of Latham's hands together above his head, and he clamped his left wrist tight around them and held them together in a vice-like grip. He placed his right hand around Latham's throat and started to squeeze.

Latham was helpless in The Kid's powerful hold. He could not do anything to defend himself and his face started to change colour to a shade of purple. Latham's eyes began to bulge as Sundance increased his pressure on the lawman's throat.

Latham started to writhe on the ground.

Johnny felt sickened at what he was watching. Joe Latham was corrupt, but he was still his father.

Seated on the bench on the porch next to Hank and Louisa, Rosa felt a little unsure at what Sundance was doing, but she tried to keep her trust in The Kid. Louisa looked away with a gasp of horror and disgust.

Hank wisely said to her, 'Sundance will have his reasons for what he's doing to Latham, you can be sure of that.'

Deputy Jeb Taylor suddenly shouted out that somebody should put a stop to what Sundance was doing but Butch told him to shut up.

Johnny was standing to one side of Butch while keeping hold of Wade Ashton, and Butch sensed that the boy was about to interfere. He saw Johnny let go of Ashton's arm and reach down to his holster for his gun.

Butch did not like what he was watching either, but he trusted Sundance implicitly, and he said harshly to Johnny, 'Don't be a damn fool, Johnny. If you draw that gun and try to use it, then you'll be dead for sure; if Sundance don't see you and kill you, then I will, and your father ain't worth it!'

Butch would not hesitate to kill anyone who threatened his partner.

Johnny realized that Butch was right. His father was not worth it. Since they had taken over the ranch, Butch and Sundance were always there for him, but his father never had been.

Johnny took his hand away from his

gun and said in an apologetic tone to Butch, 'I never would have used the gun ... and you are right, my father ain't worth it.'

Sundance released his hold on Latham's throat, and the marshal started spluttering and gasping in air.

'Do you surrender?' The Kid asked calmly.

Latham did not say anything.

The Kid started to squeeze the law-man's throat again, but before The Kid's grip had tightened too much, Latham started to make gurgling noises.

Sundance released his grip.

'OK, OK!' Latham spluttered. 'I surrender!'

Sundance grinned. 'Say it again.'

'I surrender!' Latham spluttered again.

'Well, Latham,' Sundance said, still grinning, 'do you feel as foolish as you look? There's no fun in surrendering, is there?' He was using the same words that the marshal had used with Butch.

Latham lay making choking sounds and gasping as Sundance let go of his wrists and stood up.

Butch smiled to himself when he heard The Kid's words to Latham. He knew that Sundance had done it for him, but it did not give him much pleasure; he could not take any joy from someone else's pain.

He was glad it was over.

Latham closed his eyes and gulped in air, he was apparently unable to move.

Sundance stood watching him; he did not trust the man.

Rosa called out to The Kid from the bench where she sat on the porch saying something about fetching some rope for him to use to tie Latham up with, and she hurried away to the stables.

For a fraction of a second, Sundance turned to look at her and his attention was away from Latham. The lawman's eyes suddenly shot open and his right hand snaked down to his belt and he yanked out a gun that he had hidden down there. He started to get hurriedly to his knees.

Butch saw Latham's movements and

he yelled out a warning to his partner while pulling out his own Colt. As he did so, a group of riders were approaching the ranch house, but no one had seen or heard them.

At Butch's warning, and in a lightning fast movement, The Kid spun round on Latham. He drew his Colt at the same time, and before the marshal who was now on his knees and aiming at Sundance could pull the trigger, two bullets slammed into him, and he staggered backwards.

The first bullet to hit Latham came from The Kid's Colt; it tore straight through his heart, killing him instantly. The Kid's bullet was rapidly followed by a bullet from Butch's Colt, which ploughed through the lawman's chest. The impact of the two bullets jerked Latham backwards and blood poured out from the two wounds. A vacant look was in Latham's eyes and he started to topple over, and then a third bullet from an unknown shooter struck Latham in the forehead. The marshal spun round and pitched forward on to his face.

Blood started to form a pool around his lifeless body.

Johnny turned away with a gulp, and Rosa, who had returned with the rope, rushed over to him and hugged him. She partly blamed herself for distracting Sundance.

Deputies Taylor and Ashton looked at each other with grim expressions.

Then all at once, it seemed, they all turned to look at the man who had fired the third bullet into Latham, and who had taken them all by surprise. He had ridden up to the ranch house with some other men at the moment that Latham had got to his knees and was about to shoot Sundance. No one had seen or heard the approach of him and his men because they had all been so engrossed in what was taking place with Sundance and Latham.

'Jacob!' Butch shouted happily on recognizing his friend, Jacob Hurley, the governor of Wyoming.

Hurley dismounted to shake hands

with Butch and Sundance. He gave them both swift hugs, which Sundance tried to pull away from. Butch laughed at his partner.

'It's good to see you both,' Hurley smiled.

The governor was a small, jolly-looking man with brown hair and a moustache. The two outlaws were his friends, and he owed them a lot. They had once helped him out of a very dangerous situation when he had been captured by a gang of vicious bandits.

Hurley glanced at Deputies Taylor and Ashton, who stood looking grim and nervous with their hands tied, and he said, 'I see that I have two prisoners to take back with me.'

The governor then tipped his hat to Rosa and had a few words with young Johnny, who was still upset about his father's death.

'What are you doing here?' Butch asked as Hurley turned back to him.

'I came to speak to you about the pardon.'

Sundance asked the governor rather curtly, 'What chance do we have for a pardon now? I just killed a US marshal.'

'Latham got what he deserved,' Hurley scoffed with a smile at his two friends. 'He was a disgrace to his badge. I think you did us all a favour, and anyway, you only had a part of a kill. I'll put it in my report that I killed him, and I have witnesses.' He turned and indicated the three men who had ridden up with him, and who were all still seated on their horses.

'They are all lawmen,' he explained to Butch and Sundance, 'and they will back my story — no true law officer liked Joe Latham.'

Butch smiled, he was happy and thankful at what Jacob had said.

Hurley went back to Johnny to speak to him some more and to offer what comfort he could. The boy was still very distressed.

Hank got up from the bench where he had been sitting next to Louisa. He stepped forward and invited everyone into the ranch house for a meal. His invite was gratefully accepted.

As the others slowly piled into the ranch house with Hank, taking with them their still tied up prisoners, Butch, Sundance, and Johnny were left on their own.

Johnny approached Sundance nervously and said, 'I'm sorry I almost interfered, but I did trust you in the end.'

The Kid gave him an impassive look, and said sharply, 'You still got a long way to go to gain any trust from me, Johnny.'

The boy nodded sadly and walked away.

Butch stared at The Kid's cut and blood-stained face; his partner had obviously taken a lot of a pounding from Latham, and his knuckles were blood-smeared. 'Are you OK?' Butch asked anxiously.

'Just a few scratches,' Sundance answered in his usual curt way.

Butch sighed. 'Are you sure?' he asked; he knew that Sundance would never admit to being hurt or in pain.

'Yeah.' The Kid grinned. 'I enjoyed

giving Latham a beating.'

Butch relaxed, The Kid's grin told him that his partner had not been badly hurt.

They both took a glance at Latham's dead body.

'Jacob was right,' Butch remarked, 'he was a disgrace to his badge.'

'And,' The Kid added meaningfully, 'he was right about him getting what he deserved.'

Butch grinned, and there was no reproach in his voice when he said, 'He certainly got that, partner.'

Sundance smiled, one of his rare, self-satisfied smiles, then he said quietly, 'I hope I haven't ruined our chances of getting a pardon.' He knew that Butch was really hoping that they could get a pardon, and be able to just concentrate on their ranch. He was not as bothered about it as Butch was, but he was proud of their ranch, and he had not missed robbing any banks or trains, or residing at Hole-in-the-Wall.

Butch squeezed The Kid's arm. 'You did what you had to do. I'm not sorry that you killed Latham, or that I helped you to do it. I'm glad that it's him that's dead and not you, and anyway, you heard what Jacob said; he'll take the blame for Latham's death.'

Butch then slid his arm around The Kid's shoulders and started to steer him towards the ranch house. 'Let's go inside and eat,' he said.

It was much later that afternoon after they had all enjoyed a meal cooked for them by Hank, Rosa, and Louisa, when Butch noticed that Louisa was looking upset, and she discreetly made an exit from the ranch house. Butch followed her into one of the barns.

Louisa was sitting in the hayloft when Butch joined her. She had been crying.

'What's wrong?' he asked her gently.

Louisa said, 'I guess it's all just got too much for me — all that trouble with Abe ... and now all this ... ' Her voice trailed off.

'You have had a tough time of it,' Butch agreed.

'I'm not like Rosa,' Louisa sniffed. 'She's very strong.'

Butch gave her a hug.

Louisa said, 'What Sundance did to Latham was sick.'

'He had his reasons.'

'That's what Hank said, but I think that he was cruel.' Louisa's voice was unsteady. 'It was so awful to watch.'

Butch did not like talking about his partner when he was not there, but he felt that he had to say something in The Kid's defence, so he said, 'There is a very vicious, even sadistic streak in Sundance, you've known him long enough to know that, but he has to be pushed a long way before he'll ever show it, and Latham pushed him just that little bit too far.'

'You mean because Latham tried to hang him?' Louisa asked.

'No, not because of that,' Butch said quietly. 'Sundance could handle that…' He hesitated before saying, 'It's because of what Latham did to me, he hurt me very badly … he tortured me in a way.'

Louisa looked at him in alarm.

Butch said quickly, 'And that's all I'll ever say about it.' He had not wanted to tell her, but he did not want her to think that Sundance had enjoyed almost torturing the marshal.

Louisa cried out, 'Oh, Butch, I'm so sorry!'

'We'll not mention this again,' Butch said sternly. 'I only told you because I don't want you to think that Sundance enjoys being cruel. I know him better than anyone, and he does not.'

'I'm sorry,' Louisa said again; she always seemed to say or do the wrong thing with Butch.

'Sundance is a true friend,' Butch said to her, 'just remember that.'

She nodded. 'I know that.'

They climbed down from the hayloft, and Butch smiled at her and took her hand as they left the barn. They started to walk back to the ranch house, and on the way they saw Sundance and Jacob Hurley standing near the fence of one of the horse corrals talking together.

Butch let go of Louisa's hand and

went over to join them. The five young horses in the corral all trotted over to greet Butch at the fence. He stroked them all and then turned to Jacob Hurley as the governor started speaking to him and telling him that he had heard about how Joe Latham had tricked him into the meeting at Red Creek, and about how Latham had tried to hang both Butch and Sundance. Then Hurley said that he had good news regarding the pardon. That all the two outlaws had to do was to stay away from robbing banks and trains for a year and then there was a possibility that they might get the pardon.

Hurley smiled affectionately at them both as he said, 'That's the reason I put a bullet into Latham's brain, so that it will go on my report that I killed him and not either one of you two — so it means that you've still got a chance of the pardon.'

Butch smiled. 'We're lucky to have you, Jacob.'

'Rubbish!' Hurley exclaimed. 'It's me that's lucky to have you two, and a lot of people think like me; you two have a lot of friends!'

Butch and Sundance smiled at each other.

'I'll be getting ready to leave now,' Hurley said, and he walked away from them.

Sundance started to follow the governor, but Butch stayed where he was. He leaned against one of the corral posts and thought about what the pardon meant to him.

It meant that he would be a free man in Wyoming, and that he and Sundance could run the ranch without fear of being arrested. He looked downwards as he began to think about Amy. He even began to hope that he could maybe ask her to join him and Sundance on the ranch, but then he dismissed the idea as an impossibility. It would be twelve months or more before they would even know if they had got the pardon, and there was always the danger of his restless spirit getting bored with the ranch and wanting some other excitement, and he could not put Amy through all that again. He had hurt her enough, and he knew that Amy was happy and settled with someone else.

Butch was so lost in his thoughts that he had not noticed that Sundance had walked back to him. The Kid was staring keenly at his partner — he knew what Butch was thinking about.

Butch suddenly looked up as he felt The Kid's eyes on him.

'You're thinking about Amy,' The Kid stated.

Butch smiled, it always amazed him how easily they could read each other's minds.

'Yeah,' Butch sighed, 'I had this crazy idea that if we did get the pardon, then maybe I could ask Amy to join us on the Ranch.'

'If that's what you want,' Sundance told him seriously, 'we could make it work.'

Butch smiled again with warmth in his eyes. The Kid never let him down, but then his eyes turned sad as he said, 'But like I said, it was a crazy idea. I can't put Amy through that again. She's happy now with someone else, and it'll be a year or more before we even know if we'll get the pardon, and by then we might want some more excitement — '

'Some more excitement?' Sundance began.

'I like owning the ranch,' Butch emphasized, his eyes still sad, 'and I enjoy the life we have here, but I can't control this restless spirit inside of me, and maybe, one day in the future the ranch won't be enough.'

'I know what you mean,' Sundance said in understanding. He had the same kind of adventurous spirit inside of him that Butch had.

They looked round as Jacob Hurley re-joined them. He said that he and his men were leaving. He promised to keep in touch regarding the progress of the pardon. Hurley took with him his two prisoners, Deputies Jeb Taylor and Wade Ashton, and he also took Joe Latham's dead body. He told Johnny that he would arrange a proper burial for the marshal.

7

Over two weeks had passed since the incident with Joe Latham when Rosa asked Sundance to give her some more training with a gun. The Kid had agreed to it although he did not think that she needed any more training.

They rode into one of the canyons on the opposite side of the river. Before giving Rosa some training, The Kid did some practising of his own.

Rosa watched in awe as he placed a coin on the back of his hand, then he tilted his hand until the coin started to fall off, he whipped his hand down to grab his gun butt, pulled out his Colt, and, shooting from the hip, he blasted a hole through the coin before it hit the ground. He repeated this several times and his speed was phenomenal.

Sundance then tossed some coins in the air for Rosa to shoot at.

After he had watched her shooting at the coins, Sundance said, 'You don't need any more training, Rosa.'

'Don't you think so?' Rosa asked him. She sounded disappointed.

She was happy that he thought she could shoot well enough, but she was sad at the thought of having no more lessons from him. She liked spending time alone with him.

Sundance gave her a strange look. 'You can shoot well enough now to protect yourself,' he told her, 'and Abe Gannon ain't a problem to you no more.'

Rosa nodded. She hated the casual way he always treated her, and the way that her heart always flipped over when he looked at her.

Sundance suddenly caught the way that she was looking at him, and he wondered if he had done something or said something to upset her. It never occurred to him that she might have some loving feelings for him. He thought she liked Johnny.

Rosa was standing close to the edge of

the canyon cliff face, and she had to lower her head as she found herself blushing as he looked at her. Forgetting how close to the edge of the cliff she stood, she stepped back. She lost her footing, teetered on the edge for half a second, and then with a startled cry, she fell.

The Kid frantically tried to grab her, but missed. He looked over the edge of the cliff and let out a gasp of relief when he saw her clinging to a shrub a few feet below him. He was about to spring over to where his horse was tethered to fetch a rope when Rosa called up to him that she could not hold on for much longer, she could feel the shrub coming loose.

There was no time for The Kid to fetch a rope, so he quickly lowered himself over the cliff edge and climbed down carefully towards her. The cliff face was covered with huge rocks, trees and thick shrubs.

The Kid found handholds and foot-holds in crevices amongst the rocks and shrubs. He reached Rosa and grabbed hold of her left hand just as she felt the shrub that she clung to break loose.

Rosa was very frightened and Sundance could feel her trembling as he held her hand. He told her calmly to reach out with her right hand and try to find a handhold, and to climb back up the cliff face.

'I'll be right behind you,' he assured her, 'so you will not fall.'

Rosa took a few deep breaths, and tried to control her feeling of panic. His calm voice helped her, and also the feel of his hand in hers. She reached out with her right hand and found a secure handhold.

Sundance let go of her left hand and told her to start climbing up. He could have climbed alongside her, but he stayed behind her in case she slipped and fell.

Inch by inch, Rosa hauled herself up the cliff face, and Sundance found himself admiring her nerve.

There was only a couple of feet left before she reached the top of the cliff and Rosa was just inches from safety when she heard a noise behind her — it sounded like a slithering noise, like someone falling.

'Sundance?' Rosa called anxiously.

There was no answer.

Frantic with worry, Rosa scrambled the rest of the way to the top and looked down the high cliff face for some sign of Sundance.

There was none. All she could see were the huge rocks, shrubs and trees below.

Rosa screamed his name several times, but got no answer.

The cliff face stretched down for hundreds of feet and Rosa felt full of fear. Her eyes desperately scanned the terrain below her. The cliff face was covered in small trees, thick shrubs and rocks of all shapes and sizes. It was impossible to spot a person lying amongst all of that.

Rosa looked up at the sky. There was another worry: it would be dark in a few hours, and she had yet to ride back to the ranch.

Sundance had fallen about twenty feet on to a small ledge that jutted out slightly from the cliff face, and he had rolled into a recess that was just behind the ledge.

231

The recess was only narrow and about eight feet long. He had hit his head hard on the ledge when landing on it and had been knocked unconscious. He had dislodged some large chunks of rocks in his fall, and the rocks had fallen on top of the ledge. Some of the rocks had rolled on top of him in the recess making it impossible for Rosa to see him.

He had not been able to answer Rosa's frantic calls to him because he was unconscious.

Back at Bitter Creek Ranch, Louisa and Hank were having a friendly argument in the kitchen. Louisa was saying that she had a recipe for some biscuits that she wanted to try out. Hank was teasing her by saying that only he could make the best biscuits.

Hank, Rosa, and Louisa often had amicable arguments about who was the best cook on the ranch. Sundance who, strangely, liked to cook at times, often joined in their arguments.

Butch sat on the sofa in the living

room. He had found a rare, quiet moment to strum on Hank's guitar. He could play a few notes and was strumming away trying not to listen to the argument in the kitchen when Rosa burst in.

She was shaking and crying and her words were streaming out of her mouth in gulps and gasps, and no one could clearly hear what she was trying to say.

It took quite a few minutes before Butch, Hank and Louisa could calm Rosa down enough so that they could hear what she was trying to say. When Butch finally did make out her words, he felt even more frantic than she did.

There was only about an hour of daylight left when Butch, Rosa, and Johnny rode up to the canyon where Sundance had taken Rosa to give her some shooting training. They dismounted and looked over the edge of the cliff down which Sundance had disappeared.

Butch stared down at the drop that went on for hundreds of feet to the bed of the canyon, and he closed his eyes for a second as a terrible fear for his partner's life engulfed him.

Butch called out for The Kid, he called again and again, but he received no answer.

Rosa and Johnny watched him with worried faces.

Butch's heart was filled with dread at what he might find as he took his lariat from his horse and fastened one end to the trunk of a tree at the top of the cliff face. He tied the other end around his chest and the loop slipped up under his armpits as he lowered himself over the cliff.

Butch climbed down to about thirty feet which was as far as the lariat would stretch. He searched through as much area as he could. He searched around the huge rocks and small trees and through the thick bushes. He scratched his hands and face, but he did not care, and all the time he called out for his partner. He even whistled quietly their secret whistle, but silence was his only reply.

Johnny took his own rope from his

horse, and tying one end of the rope to a different tree trunk to Butch, and the other end around himself, he also climbed down the cliff. He lowered himself to about twenty feet and began to search the area around him.

Rosa waited anxiously at the top.

Dusk was starting to descend when Johnny climbed back up to join Rosa. He looked into her eyes: they both feared the worst. They feared that Sundance had fallen much further than they could ever reach with the rope. They looked down the cliff at Butch who was still frantically searching; neither one of them wanted to tell him to give up.

Eventually Johnny called, 'Butch, it's getting too dark to see anything, maybe we should ride back to the ranch, and carry on with the search tomorrow.'

Butch climbed back up the cliff face to join them, he said, 'You two can ride back to the ranch, I'm staying here.'

'For how long?' Rosa asked.

'For as long as it takes,' Butch answered in a very dejected tone. 'I ain't leaving here without Sundance.'

Johnny and Rosa looked at each other. They were concerned about Butch getting tired and hungry and they said so to him.

'I can't eat,' Butch told them, 'or sleep, or leave here without Sundance.'

Rosa grabbed his arm. 'Butch,' she said softly, 'we know how you feel … ' She was also very upset about Sundance.

Butch pulled his arm loose. 'I don't think you do,' he said, his eyes glistening with tears, 'or you'd know why I can't leave.'

Rosa asked quietly, 'Why do you have such a strong bond with Sundance?'

She knew what it was like to be close to someone — she was close to her sister — but the amazing bond of Butch and Sundance was something different, and it puzzled her. The two men were not even blood kin.

'That's private,' Butch answered her.

It was not too long after Rosa and Johnny left Butch at the canyon that night fell and it was completely black.

Butch sat at the top of the canyon wall, leaning back against a tree trunk. There was only a faint light from the moon. Butch felt distraught. Tears were still in his eyes, and he refused to believe that The Kid was dead.

The bond that he shared with Sundance was hard to explain to anyone who had not experienced such a bond. Butch and Sundance were two entirely different people; their bond had not been forged out of their own personal feelings for each other, but out of exceptional circumstances. They had faced death and danger together, and had many times placed their lives in each other's hands. Sundance had eventually turned out to be the only gang member that Butch could rely on.

They had also saved each other's lives at great personal risk.

Their bond could be described as similar to a bond that soldiers shared in battle, or to that of blood brothers, but they were now, though, also family to each other.

Butch was used to sleeping out under the stars, so being alone in the canyon did not bother him. He felt tired, but he could not sleep. When it was light enough for him to see, and after first seeing to the needs of his horse, Butch tied the rope around his chest again and went down the cliff face to search for his partner. He whistled softly, but no answer came to him.

Butch felt like he had been searching for hours when he was joined by Johnny, Rosa, Louisa and Hank.

They stood at the top of the cliff looking down on him and Hank shouted down to Butch to come back up the cliff and join them, they would take over the search.

Butch shook his head.

'You are exhausted,' Hank called down. 'We are not; let us take over the search for a while.'

Butch realized that Hank was talking sense. He did feel exhausted and it was not only from lack of sleep and searching. Worry for The Kid had completely drained his strength. Grabbing hold of the rope, Butch climbed wearily back up to the top of the cliff.

Hank offered him some food that he had brought with him, but Butch refused it, he would not take a drink of water either. He again sat back against a tree trunk and watched as Hank and Johnny tied their ropes around the trunks of neighbouring trees, looped the ropes around their chests, and went down the cliff face to search.

Time passed and still Hank and Johnny carried on searching. They tirelessly searched through the thick undergrowth, around the trees, and around the rocks calling out Sundance's name.

Rosa and Louisa stood near to Butch. Rosa was quietly sobbing. She felt that it was all her fault. Louisa put an arm around her sister and tried to console her.

Hank and Johnny climbed back up the cliff to get a drink of water from their canteens. They had left them at the top while they searched, and as they drank from their canteens, Butch looked at their faces and he could see that they did not think that they would find Sundance alive.

'Sundance ain't dead,' Butch told them weakly, 'I know he ain't.'

Hank said with a smile, 'Well, if you think that, then so do we...We'll search for as long as you want us to.'

Hank meant what he had said. He had known Butch and Sundance for a lot of years. He had been an outlaw at Hole-in-the-Wall, and he knew that Butch and Sundance had never let their friends down, and he did not intend to let them down now.

Johnny, Rosa, and Louisa all felt the same. They would be there for as long as Butch needed them. Butch and Sundance had always been there for them.

Johnny felt particularly bad about almost choosing his father over the two outlaws. Louisa had told Johnny and Rosa about what Butch had said to her about how Joe Latham had tortured him in a way. Johnny and Rosa had been horrified, and all three of them had agreed to keep it amongst themselves.

The day dragged on and so did the search.

Butch lowered his head as tears again filled his eyes. He felt weak, nauseous and in despair, but he would not leave the canyon without his partner, no matter how long it took.

Rosa and Louisa looked at him anxiously.

Hank suddenly shouted out, 'I heard something!'

Butch lifted his head and got unsteadily to his feet. His heart started to thump rapidly as he dared to hope. He wiped away his tears on his shirt sleeve.

Everyone stood still, hardly daring to breathe as they listened intently.

They heard nothing.

'I'm sure I heard something,' Hank said looking up at Butch. 'It sounded like a low moan.'

Butch desperately called out his partner's name.

Only silence answered him.

'Tell us where you are, partner!' Butch yelled frantically.

Sundance had remained unconscious all night as Butch sat at the top of the canyon wall. He had come round for a few minutes early that morning and he had heard Butch whistling to him, but he had passed out again before he could attempt to answer.

The Kid returned to consciousness once more and heard movement quite close to him. He was lying on his stomach in the recess with rocks covering him. There was dust and bits of rocks in his mouth. He felt almost crushed by the rocks on top of him. His head wound had bled a lot and he felt weak from the blood loss. He tried to call out, but only managed a faint moan, then he heard Hank's voice — it sounded very near to him — and he heard Butch desperately calling his name, and then his partner's frantic yell about telling them where he was.

Sundance tried to call out again, and he tried to move. At first he could make no sound and he could not move because of the weight of the rocks that covered him, but with determination and the super human strength that he seemed to possess, he somehow forced out a moan, and he managed to move slightly.

Hank heard the moan coming from a pile of rocks to the right of him. He noticed the slight movement, and he made his way over to them and started moving the rocks away. Butch was suddenly filled with renewed strength and hope, and he tied the rope around his chest again and climbed down to help Hank. Johnny scrambled over to help them too, and the three men tore away the rocks and found Sundance lying in the recess.

'Oh, Sundance, thank God!' Butch gasped out when he saw his partner, and he started to keel over with relief. He almost vomited.

Hank had to reach out a hand to steady Butch, and then they carefully pulled The Kid out. Sundance's eyes flickered open and he tried to acknowledge Butch with a smile, but he lapsed into unconsciousness again.

He was covered in dust and pieces of

rock. Hank put his ear to The Kid's chest and heard a faint heartbeat. He checked Sundance over; one side of his head was matted with blood and there was a deep gash on his leg, but he did not appear to have any broken bones.

Standing at the top of the cliff face, Rosa and Louisa hugged each other with relief.

Butch, Hank, and Johnny managed between them to carry the unconscious Sundance up to the top of the cliff face while holding on to their ropes with just one hand.

Although exhausted, Butch held his inert partner in front of him on his horse as they all rode back to the ranch. Once back at the ranch house, Sundance was taken up to his bedroom, which Rosa was currently using.

Butch helped Hank to tend to The Kid's wounds and to change him into some clean clothes. They cleaned and bandaged The Kid's head and leg wounds. The bleeding had stopped, but he had obviously lost a lot of blood. His clothes had been drenched with it in places. They were careful not to start the bleeding again.

Butch sank down in a chair next to the bed, he still felt worried sick. Hank said to him, 'Don't worry. I'm sure he'll be fine, but he'll have to stay still for a few days, he's lost a lot of blood and we can't risk his head wound opening up again.'

Sundance stirred and moaned on the bed, and his eyes slowly opened. His eyes did not focus properly at first and he looked confused.

'Hi, partner.' Butch smiled warmly at him. 'How d'you feel?'

Sundance's eyes started to focus and as his confusion faded, he gave Butch a weak smile of recognition. Although feeling weak and in pain, Sundance still noticed how weary Butch looked. He knew instinctively how desperately worried his partner must have been, because he knew how he would have felt in Butch's place.

'I could do with a whiskey,' Sundance murmured in answer to Butch's question. His voice sounded weak compared to the normal strong, expressive voice that he had.

Hank left the room to fetch a glass of whiskey for Sundance and some food. After having a few sips of whiskey and eating a small amount of food, Sundance started to fall asleep.

Hank had given some food to Butch as well, but Butch only ate a few mouthfuls.

'You look exhausted,' Sundance murmured sleepily to his partner after Hank had left them alone again. 'Why don't you go and get some sleep? I ain't going anywhere.'

'I'm staying right here,' Butch insisted. He would not leave his partner until he felt sure that The Kid was going to be all right, and that his head wound would not start bleeding again.

The next morning, Sundance awoke feeling much better. His head hurt and so did his leg, and most of his body ached, but he felt a lot stronger.

His eyes focused on Butch in the chair. His partner was still asleep and The Kid noticed that Butch's face was a sickly pale colour, and he looked completely worn out. Sundance felt concerned for him.

Hank entered the bedroom. He gently woke Butch up, and told him to go and eat some food, and to get some proper rest.

'Do as he says,' Sundance said, still speaking in a weak murmur, 'I don't need a nursemaid.'

Butch insisted on staying where he was.

Hank sighed, and asked Butch, 'Do you want me to have two patients on my hands?'

Butch did not answer. He would not leave Sundance until he felt completely sure that The Kid was going to pull through. His partner's weak voice worried him.

Hank gave up with Butch, and he turned to The Kid and said firmly, 'You'll have to stay put in that bed for a few days and not move about too much. We can't risk your head wound opening up again.'

Sundance hated just lying around and murmured, 'I'm not too sure about that.'

'You'll have to,' Butch said, his voice also firm. 'You've lost too much blood already ... If you try to move from that bed, I'll tie you in it, that's what you said to me, ain't it?'

Sundance smiled slightly, he said to Butch in a much stronger voice, 'I'll stay put on one condition: that you, *amigo*, do as Hank says, and go and get some food and some proper rest.'

Butch smiled. He felt happier on hearing the strong tone in Sundance's voice. Some colour returned to his face. 'It's a deal, partner,' he said.

8

Just over four weeks later, Jasper and Jesse Sheldon held a dance to celebrate the opening of their saloon, which they had named 'The Big Horn Saloon' after the Big Horn mountain range.

The dance was being held inside the saloon, and also in a huge barn to the right of the saloon.

Residents from the nearby towns and ranches, and some outlaws from Hole-in-the-Wall were enjoying the dance along with Butch, Sundance, Johnny, Rosa, and Louisa, and some other ranch-hands.

Inside the saloon, there was a man playing the piano while some men and ladies danced. Inside the huge barn next to the saloon, some chairs and tables had been placed, and a couple of men were playing fiddles. A few people were dancing to the tunes that the fiddlers were playing. The doors of the barn were open wide.

Butch bought most of his friends inside the saloon a drink. He was very popular with almost everyone because of his generosity. When he finally managed to get away from them he went inside the barn with Louisa, and they sat at a table together watching the dancers.

Louisa said to Butch, 'Rosa and I are thinking of leaving the ranch next week. We'll be staying with relatives in Casper.'

Butch said, 'We'll miss you.'

'Will you?'

'Of course,' Butch replied with a smile, but he added quickly, not wanting to give her false hope about his feelings for her, 'you two are our friends.'

'Can we visit you?' Louisa asked.

'Anytime.' Butch smiled again, then he said seriously, 'You don't have to leave, but if you want the life that you told me about, you won't find it by staying with us.'

'I know,' Louisa sighed.

They were silent for a while, then Louisa asked, 'Do you think that you will stay out of trouble for a year, and maybe get the pardon?'

'I don't know,' Butch answered truthfully. 'I never try to plan the future. I told you before, Louisa, I have a restless spirit; I like being a rancher at the moment, so does Sundance. I'd like to think we'll get the pardon, and we'll keep the ranch for a few years, but … '

'Your restless spirit?'

He grinned, 'Yeah.'

'You always say 'we',' Louisa remarked in a puzzled tone. 'When you talk about the future … don't you see a future without him in it?'

'Who?'

'Sundance, of course.'

'Oh.' Butch looked at her a bit taken aback, then he asked her, 'Do you see a future without Rosa in it?'

'No, but that's different, Rosa is my blood kin.'

Butch smiled. 'In my mind, Sundance is my blood kin. We are as close as two brothers could ever be. In a way, I guess we are closer — he's never let me down, and I know I'll never let him down — and no, I don't see a future without him in it in some way.'

They both started to watch the dancing.

The fiddlers were playing a lively polka, and Louisa looked surprised as she saw Sundance and Rosa whirling around with the other dancers in the barn. They were doing the steps really well and keeping time with the music.

'I can't believe he can dance like that!' Louisa said in amazement.

Butch laughed. 'Oh, he cooks too!'

'I know he can cook,' Louisa smiled.

The Kid often cooked them all breakfast at the ranch, he even cooked for Hank and the other ranch-hands.

'He has a good singing voice too,' Butch carried on. 'You should hear him singing to the cattle sometimes at night to calm them. A man of many talents and surprises is my partner.'

Louisa laughed and she realized how much she would miss the two outlaws, especially Butch, whose sparkling blue eyes filled her with a strong desire for him. She wondered if she would ever find anyone like him.

They watched Sundance and Rosa still happily doing the polka together, and then the music changed, the fiddlers started to play a slow tune. Sundance still held Rosa in his arms in a dance hold and she moved up closer to him so that she was almost touching his body with her own. She wanted him to draw her even closer to him, but instead of doing that, he suddenly let go of her, and he turned and walked away. He left Rosa standing looking very dismayed as the other dancers carried on dancing to the slow tune.

Luckily for Rosa, Johnny rushed up to her, and took her eagerly into his arms to dance with her.

Louisa said in disbelief to Butch, 'Did you see what he did?'

'Yeah.' Butch could not help but laugh. 'I told you he was a man of many surprises. He's definitely a one-off.' He said the words with pride and affection.

Ranch-hand Mark Casey came up to

the table, and took Louisa off for a dance. Sundance strolled over to join Butch. He sat down in the chair recently vacated by Louisa, and Butch smiled at him.

'So, have you bought everyone a drink yet?' Sundance asked Butch with a hint of teasing in his voice.

The Kid knew how generous Butch was with his money.

Before Butch could answer, Sundance took a quick look around him. 'Oh, you must have done,' he stated with mischief in his eyes, 'there's no-one hanging around you.'

'Oh, very funny.' Butch smiled, then he said reproachfully, 'You shouldn't treat a lady that way, partner, especially one as pretty and as brave as Rosa.'

'How'd I treat her?'

'You left her standing alone in the middle of a dance.'

'Oh,' Sundance grinned, 'I'm sure she'd rather dance with Johnny.'

Butch sighed deeply; Sundance still had not noticed how Rosa felt about him. 'Why do you think that?' he asked.

'She likes Johnny.'

Butch shook his head. 'No, partner, it's Johnny who likes her.'

Sundance shrugged. 'That's the same thing.'

'You knucklehead!' Butch almost yelled at him although affection was in his eyes. 'It is not the same thing at all. Rosa likes someone else!'

'Who?' Sundance asked in surprise.

'Oh, gosh!' Butch almost yelled again. He pretended to take thought. 'That's a tough one!'

The Kid looked into Butch's eyes, and then as usual, he read his partner's mind.

'No', he said, 'you're wrong, Rosa can't possibly like me. Anyway, she's just a kid.'

'Rosa does like you,' Butch told him. 'She has always liked you, and she's not thirteen any more, or hadn't you noticed that?'

Sundance was silent, thinking it over, then he grinned. 'So that's why you asked me to give her some training with a gun. I knew you were up to something.'

The following week, Rosa and Louisa left the ranch to stay with their relatives in Casper. They were missed by everyone on the ranch, even The Kid although he would never admit it.

About a month later, Louisa rode up to the ranch house just as Butch was coming out the door.

'I came for a visit,' she said as she dismounted. She had missed him terribly after only a few weeks.

Butch took her in his arms to give her a quick hug. 'It's a long ride from Casper,' he said.

'It is,' Louisa smiled, 'but we stayed at a few neighbouring ranches on the way here.'

'We?' Butch asked. 'Is Rosa here too?'

'Yes she is,' Louisa still smiled. 'She stopped by the cattle enclosure to speak to Johnny.'

'You can stay for as long as you like,' Butch smiled at her. 'You don't have to rush back.'

Louisa lost her smile and she looked a little sad as she said, 'We'll stay overnight, but we can't stay for too long; we'll be moving to California — we have other relatives there.'

Before Butch could say anything to her, they heard the sound of approaching hoof beats and they saw Rosa riding up to them. Butch helped Rosa down from her horse and he also gave her a quick hug.

Sundance came out of the ranch house door in time to see Butch giving a hug to Rosa. He was pleased to see Rosa and Louisa, but he did not show it. He gave a brief greeting to them and went to walk on past, saying something about having some horses to train.

Rosa called him back and asked him if there was the possibility of a quick shooting lesson.

'You can shoot,' Sundance told her very impolitely, 'you don't need another lesson.'

Butch looked at Louisa, sighed and shook his head.

'Maybe we could go for a ride,' Rosa suggested. His rude manner had not put her off.

'I'm busy,' was Sundance's abrupt reply. 'And your horse is tired.'

Butch intervened. 'Go and find Rosa a fresh horse, partner,' he said with a bright smile, 'and go for a ride with her, it's the least you can do now that she has ridden all the way from Casper for a visit.'

'If she has ridden all that way,' Sundance's voice did not soften, 'she might want to rest.'

Butch still smiled brightly as he said, 'Well, take the buggy. Go for a picnic with her.'

They had a doctor's type buggy with a folding top in the stables.

Sundance stared at him for a moment, his face was impassive, and then he snapped at his partner, saying harshly, 'Don't tell me what to do!'

Butch lowered his head. He had asked for that in a way. Sundance would not take too much teasing.

The Kid immediately regretted snapping at Butch as he remembered his partner's sensitive side and he said, 'Sorry I snapped, but you should know better.'

Butch lifted his head and smiled at The Kid. 'Yeah, I should,' he said. Sundance turned away and headed towards one of the horse corrals.

Rosa called him back again.

He stopped and turned to look at her and he was on the point of saying something harsh to her too when he noticed for the first time the soft glow in her dark brown eyes and how pretty she was, and he knew that he had missed her.

Rosa started to smile at him and she said, 'This is probably our first and last visit. We are going to stay with some other relatives in California. Surely you have time for a quick buggy ride?'

Sundance's voice had softened as he said, 'Well, I guess we could take the buggy and have a quick ride... '

Butch smiled at Louisa.

Sundance went into the stables to get the buggy, and Butch went into the ranch house to speak to Hank. He came back out after a few minutes with a picnic basket, which he handed to Rosa. 'Have a good day,' he smiled at her.

They heard the low rumble of wheels as Sundance came out of the stables seated on the buggy. He had hitched a young Quarter Horse to the vehicle. He pulled the horse to a stop near to where they stood. Rosa climbed into the seat beside him and he saw the picnic basket in her hands. He glared at Butch.

A very mischievous smile lit up Butch's face as he said, 'Aw, Kid, don't snap at me again, just go and have some fun. You heard Rosa say they are moving to California.'

Slowly the glare left Sundance's face. He did not want to snap at Butch again, but he said impassively, 'OK … I'll go and have some fun, and I'll leave all the work for you to do, shall I?'

Butch nodded 'Yes sir.'

Butch and Louisa watched as Sundance gave the Quarter Horse a light slap with the reins. The buggy started to rumble away. The rumbling sound of the wheels was combined with the clip-clop of the horse's hoofs as Sundance gave another light slap with the reins to spur the horse on past the corrals.

'Hey, partner,' Butch called to The Kid, 'stay away from any cliff edges!'

Sundance pulled back on the reins to stop the horse, and he looked back at Butch and Louisa. Butch smiled and waved to him. He smiled again and with a lot of warmth in his smile when The Kid waved back to him.

Butch turned to Louisa and put an arm around her shoulders to lead her into the ranch house. 'I seem to remember,' he said to her, 'that you said you had a recipe for making some biscuits.'

We do hope that you have enjoyed reading this large print book.

Did you know that all of our titles are available for purchase?

We publish a wide range of high quality large print books including:
Romances, Mysteries, Classics
General Fiction
Non Fiction and Westerns

Special interest titles available in large print are:
The Little Oxford Dictionary
Music Book, Song Book
Hymn Book, Service Book

Also available from us courtesy of Oxford University Press:
Young Readers' Dictionary
(large print edition)
Young Readers' Thesaurus
(large print edition)

For further information or a free brochure, please contact us at:
Ulverscroft Large Print Books Ltd.,
The Green, Bradgate Road, Anstey,
Leicester, LE7 7FU, England.
Tel: (00 44) **0116 236 4325**
Fax: (00 44) **0116 234 0205**

Other titles in the
Linford Western Library:

DEATH MOUNTAIN

Dale Brandon

After the brutal murder of their employer, Matt Stone and Spider McCaw are determined to track down the culprits. Their search leads them to an outlaw hideout — in the area known as Death Mountain, because nobody attempting to pass has ever come back. The two friends must contend with not only the perilous mountain heights, but also a terrifying menace in a narrow canyon. Can they survive the treacherous journey and bring the killers to justice?

THE SECRET OF THE SILVER STAR

Amos Carr

Outlaw Vince Lange hides a deadly secret: he is really Deputy Marshal Charlie Dane, working undercover to bring down the Carlin gang. When a heavy snowstorm traps the bandits in their hideout, life becomes even more difficult for Dane when Frank Carlin sends him and another outlaw to fetch supplies — but only Dane returns, leaving three bodies and a burned-out ranch behind. Deciding to split the gang and head for the nearest town, Carlin gives Dane a terrible task to complete . . .